SKINNY-DIPPING
DIPPING
AT MONSTER LAKE

Books by Bill Wallace:

The Backward Bird Dog
Beauty
The Biggest Klutz in Fifth Grade
Blackwater Swamp
Buffalo Gal
The Christmas Spurs
Coyote Autumn
Danger in Quicksand Swamp
Danger on Panther Peak
[Original title: Shadow on the Snow]
A Dog Called Kitty
Eye of the Great Bear
Ferret in the Bedroom, Lizards in the Fridge
The Final Freedom
Goosed!
Journey into Terror
Never Say Quit
Red Dog
Skinny-Dipping at Monster Lake
Snot Stew
Totally Disgusting!
Trapped in Death Cave

True Friends
Upchuck and the Rotten Willy
Upchuck and the Rotten Willy: The Great Escape
Upchuck and the Rotten Willy: Running Wild
Watchdog and the Coyotes

Books by Carol and Bill Wallace:

The Flying Flea, Callie, and Me
That Furball Puppy and Me
Chomps, Flea, and Gray Cat (That's Me!)
Bub Moose
Bub, Snow, and the Burly Bear Scare
The Meanest Hound Around

Books by Nikki Wallace:

Stubby and the Puppy Pack
Stubby and the Puppy Pack to the Rescue

Available from Simon & Schuster

SKINNY-DIPPING

AT MONSTER LAKE

BILL WALLACE

ALADDIN PAPERBACKS
New York   London   Toronto   Sydney

First Aladdin Paperbacks edition August 2004
Copyright © 2003 by Bill Wallace

ALADDIN PAPERBACKS
An imprint of Simon & Schuster Children's Publishing Division
1230 Avenue of the Americas, New York, NY 10020

Also available in a Simon & Schuster Books for Young Readers hardcover edition.
Designed by O'Lanso Gabbidon
The text of this book was set in Garamond.
Manufactured in the United States of America
10 9 8 7 6 5 4

The Library of Congress has cataloged the hardcover edition as follows:
Wallace, Bill, 1947–
Skinny-dipping at Monster Lake / Bill Wallace.—1st ed.
p. cm.
Summary: When twelve-year-old Kent helps his father in a daring underwater rescue, he wins the respect he has always craved.
ISBN 0-689-85150-2 (hc.)
[1. Rescues—Fiction. 2. Lakes—Fiction. 3. Fathers and sons—Fiction.]
I. Title.
PZ7.W15473 Sk 2003
[Fic]—dc21   2002152820
ISBN-13: 978-0-689-85151-3 (Aladdin pbk.)
ISBN-10: 0-689-85151-0 (Aladdin pbk.)

To Keith Wallace, Chuck Gardner, and Gary Gardner

SKINNY-DIPPING
DIPPING
AT MONSTER LAKE

I

The sound knifed through the morning air like fingernails scraping on a chalkboard. The gentle swish of the summer breeze, the soft peaceful rhythm of waves lapping on the shore, the steady *clip clop* of horses' hooves—all were shattered by the awful screeching sound.

The scream sent a chill up my spine. I shuddered. Duke shied. I had to grab the saddle horn to keep from sliding off his back. The little hairs at the base of my neck tingled. I pulled Duke's reins. Heard him snort when he stopped. And . . .

For just an instant I almost knew how General Custer and the Seventh Cavalry must have felt when the Sioux screamed their war cries and thundered down on them.

Then . . .

The scream came again.

"You boys get out of here!"

With a tug on Duke's reins, I turned him and headed back the way we came. I don't know what made me glance over my shoulder. Well—I guess I

did know. Jordan and I had been next-door neighbors ever since we moved to Cedar Lake. I knew
him. That's why I looked back.

Sure enough, he was still headed toward the
shore.

"Jordan."

Resting the book he was reading on his saddle
horn, he didn't look up. I sucked in a deep breath.

"JORDAN!"

His head snapped. Startled, he blinked a couple
of times, then, with a finger, shoved his glasses up
on the bridge of his nose.

"Huh? What?"

"This way."

"Why?" He frowned. "We're supposed to find
the rest of our unit."

"I know, but we have to go around." With a nod
I motioned toward the rickety old boathouse.
"Mrs. Baum. Didn't you hear her screaming at us?"

Jordan shrugged. "Not really." He pointed
down at the book. "Do you know that one coaxial
cable can carry up to 132,000 conversations simul-
taneously?"

"Come on, Jordan," I said with a sigh. Jordan
was the only guy I knew who read books while he
was riding his horse.

He frowned at Mrs. Baum over the top of his

glasses and gave a little snort. "The Seventh Cavalry wouldn't run from some batty old hermit. Especially a crazy old woman like her."

"Come on, Jordan."

Reluctantly he tugged on Mac's right rein. They turned and trotted after Duke and me.

Jordan was right. What kind of cavalry officer would turn tail and run from some old grouch like Mrs. Baum? Maybe I just wasn't officer material, after all. I'd probably be an embarrassment to the whole unit.

Okay. So we really weren't the Seventh Cavalry. We weren't even cavalry, if you wanted to get technical about it. We were just a bunch of guys who lived around Cedar Lake and had horses.

Jordan came up with the name—The Seventh Cavalry—because there were seven of us. Well, there were seven until Foster moved in. But Seventh Cavalry sounded better than Eighth Cavalry.

I mean, who ever heard of the Eighth Cavalry?

Chet Bently knew nearly everything there was to know about history. He said there *was* an Eighth Cavalry. But he also said the Seventh Cavalry was the most famous mounted division in history. General George Armstrong Custer. Battle of the Little Big

Horn. Chet said everybody knew about that. He was into history, like, big time. Straight A's in class and even made it a point to straighten Mrs. Oden out if she got some of her facts mixed up. Zane Parker didn't like history. His dad did, though. He'd overheard his father talking about General Custer and those guys, so when Jordan came up with the name, Chet and Zane wouldn't even consider some of the other suggestions. From that day on, we were the Seventh Cavalry.

Daniel Shift would be the general. There was no doubt in my mind about that. He always had to be the leader—the guy in charge. Daniel was popular and rich, both.

Jordan would vote for me. If we could keep his attention long enough for him to vote. Next to Ted Aikman, Jordan was probably my best friend. Jordan could be kind of weird at times. Once when I was complaining about him, Mom said: "He just marches to a different drummer." I wasn't sure what that meant, but it probably had something to do with Jordan always having his mind on computers or reading something, instead of paying attention to what everyone else in the world was doing at the time.

Anyway, Jordan would vote for me. Chet would vote for Daniel. They were next-door neighbors.

Pepper would probably vote for him, too, as would Zane. That only left Foster. He was the wild card. Foster was usually on my team, when we divided up for sports or wars or stuff. He didn't like it much, though. That's 'cause we usually lost.

Course Foster didn't like much of anything. He especially hated his name. It used to be Foster DeJarno. Then his mom and dad got a divorce. His mom remarried a guy she used to work with named Cliff Foster. When he legally adopted Foster, that made his name Foster Foster. (I couldn't help but grin every time I thought about it.) Anyway, Foster Foster could go either direction. If I got to him first and convinced him to vote for me . . . well . . .

That would give us a four to four vote. Maybe we could think of some kind of competition to break the tie, and I could beat Daniel. Maybe . . .

Jordan snapped me from my daydreams about being general of the Seventh Cavalry. He rode past me, swung down from his horse, and started to open the gate.

"Jordan."

He lifted the wire from the top post. I took a deep breath.

"Jordan!"

Shoving his glasses up on the bridge of his nose, he looked around. When he spotted me, he smiled.

"What?"

"What are you doing?"

"Opening the gate."

"Why?"

He stood there a moment with his mouth open. Finally he shrugged.

"I don't know."

Duke and I headed up the path along the fence. With one foot in the stirrup, Jordan hopped about three times, then swung his leg over Mac, and they trotted after us. Mrs. Baum never yelled if we went across the back of her place. She didn't even seem to notice, for that matter, if we practically rode through her backyard.

She just didn't want us riding between her house and the lake.

Really we didn't have to go across her place at all. We could ride a little farther west and go by way of Mr. Heart's farm. He didn't mind. But if we went that way, we had to go through five fences instead of just two. Ended up taking us twice as long. Staying down by the water was even shorter. That's why we forgot, sometimes, to ride *behind* Mrs. Baum's house.

"I always thought it was kind of weird," I said,

as much to myself as to Jordan. "I mean, if her front yard was beautiful and landscaped or something like that, I could understand. But her front yard looks terrible. There are so many gopher mounds in it—well, it looks like some little kid was playing with a toy dump truck and left hundreds of fresh dirt piles. I can't understand why she gets so bent out of shape. Can you?"

Jordan didn't answer.

"Jordan! What do you think?"

Head cocked to one side, my friend finally shrugged.

"I think they should have named it something besides Cedar Lake. I mean, every place we went on vacation last summer, we found a Cedar Lake. There's one in Kansas and one in Colorado. Montana's got a Cedar Lake, and there are two in Oregon. Most folks just call this Monster Lake, anyway. Why couldn't the people here come up with something more original? Like Loch Ness Lake. I mean, we're supposed to have a monster living in the lake, just like in Scotland. My father said that he saw the eyes one night when he and Mom were driving home from the movies. Why don't they just call it Monster Lake? Or Lake Nessie? Or . . ."

My mouth fell open.

For a moment I was totally lost and confused. Then I couldn't figure out why I felt that way. After all, for Jordan, it wasn't that unusual. Here I was, talking about Mrs. Baum and her ugly front yard. Naturally . . . Jordan would be thinking about something altogether different. I shook my head, closed my mouth, and kept riding.

We had to get to Foster before Daniel did. Somehow, I had to talk him into voting for me.

Duke stopped quite a ways from the gate at the far side of Mrs. Baum's place. I kicked him and he went a few steps farther, then stopped again.

I should have known—right then.

Swinging down from the saddle, I tugged at the reins and practically dragged him to the fence. Once there I reached for the wire latch on the gatepost. The second I did, I realized I was in trouble.

Duke tugged at the reins and tried to back up. My eyes flashed. Twigs snapped from a pile of brush to my left. My head jerked around, just in time to see the spear.

Ambush!

Split-second reaction was all that saved me. I jumped back, leaning to the side. The spear missed me and hit Duke in the shoulder.

Jordan and I were unarmed. We hadn't even picked a spear yet.

Another spear hit Jordan. He yelled. I saw the disgusted look on his face when he swung down from the saddle and turned to fall.

There was no time to run. I bent over and grabbed for the spear on the ground. Another spear flew from a huge cottonwood, behind me and just a little to my left.

The second one got me—right in the . . .

Well, I *was* bent over.

2

Making sure I had a good hold on Duke's reins, I dropped to my knees.

I sure didn't like it, though.

But when you're wounded, you have to fall. Once on the ground, I checked around for sandburs or goatheads. Sandburs grew on stalks and were sticky, but they really didn't hurt. Goatheads were the hard, brown stickers that grew on flat vines. They were thicker than sandburs and could jab right through a thick pair of jeans. Sure it was safe, I lay down on my right side.

"It's not fair."

"You're dead. You can't talk." Daniel Shift stood over me, smiling. I glared up at him.

"I'm not dead. I'm just stuck in the . . . well, I'm just wounded. It's not fair to ambush us on Mrs. Baum's place. It's, like, off limits or something. We weren't expecting it and—"

"That's why it's called an ambush." Daniel kind of stuck his nose in the air, sneered, and wobbled his head back and forth. "An ambush comes when and *where* the enemy's not expecting it."

"It's still not fair."

"If you don't shut up, I'll finish you off." He raised his spear.

"Not fair," I mumbled under my breath.

Guess I didn't mumble it soft enough. Daniel scratched his chin. Only he didn't have much of a chin. Instead of sticking out like everyone else's chin, his kind of sloped from his bottom lip back toward his neck. Anyway, he scratched where his chin should have been. Smiled and jabbed me in the chest with his spear. I felt my lip curl when I looked up at him. Then I closed my eyes and fell limp on the ground.

"This one's dead," he boasted. There was a moment of silence, then: "This one's dead, too," Zane Parker's voice called back.

"Thousand one, thousand two, thousand three. . . ." Chet Bently began. I felt my eyes roll inside my closed eyelids. Chet Bently could count slower than anybody. It was going to take him forever to get to sixty.

I scrunched my eyes and gritted my teeth, tight as I could.

I hate being dead.

• • •

When we had first started playing "war," we'd used sunflower stalks as spears. In fact, that's what Jordan, Ted, Foster, and I still used. They worked pretty well, only they didn't fly very straight when we threw them. There was usually enough dirt on the roots that it left a spot when we hit somebody.

Last summer Daniel was watching a movie. It had this one part about army boot camp or training or something. Daniel saw these things that the army called pugil sticks. The soldiers wore football-like helmets with face masks. They used the pugil sticks sort of like a rifle—pretending one end was a bayonet and the other was the butt of the gun—then they'd try to stab or clunk each other over the head with the things. They were long sticks, padded on both ends with rubber and wrapped in canvas.

Daniel had thought they were really cool. He'd kept talking about them and pestering his dad. Mr. Shift's computer company did some stuff for the army. He talked to a couple of bigwigs on the phone, and the first thing we knew, four of these pugil sticks arrived in the mail, addressed to Daniel.

Most of the guys were on summer vacation with their folks when the things came. Daniel called on the phone, and Jordan, Zane, and I were the only ones who came. Before we even started playing with them, Zane asked why they were named pugil sticks.

We lost Jordan.

He took off and spent thirty minutes going through Daniel's Grolier Encyclopedias. When he couldn't find anything there, he hopped on his horse and rode home. About two hours later, he came back and announced that he'd found it on his computer. The word *pugilist* meant "fighter" or "boxer." So pugil sticks were sticks or clubs used to fight or box with.

He seemed real proud of himself and was ready to play. None of us cared. By then we were already worn out, bruised, and wanting to do something else.

Over the next week or so, we *did* have fun with the things. Playing army like Daniel had seen in the movie didn't work out too well. That's because, without the helmets . . . well, getting clunked in the head with those things—even though they were padded—sure gave us a headache. So after a few days we decided to use them in a different way.

We went through our "Knights of the Round Table" era. We used old, wooden baseball bats as the swords. (They were about the right size and weight. Even Sir Lancelot had to use two hands to wield his sword.) We used the pugil sticks like jousting lances.

That didn't work too hot, either.

Without a hand guard, like on a real sword, our fingers kept getting smashed. Smushed fingers ended the sword fighting *real quick.* Our horses weren't too crazy about these pugil sticks flying around their heads. When we'd charge at the other knight, the horses usually shied away and we couldn't stab anybody. On the few occasions we managed to keep our horses going straight long enough to make contact, we figured out why the knights wore all that armor. Getting knocked off a running horse and landing flat on your back in the middle of the pasture was no fun at all. We gave up on our Knights of the Round Table thing and went back to being the Seventh Cavalry.

Zane Parker's dad was a brick mason. He had boxes and boxes of this bright blue chalk. He used it to coat string that he and his crew stretched and thumped against the ground to lay out straight lines for walls and stuff. Since there was plenty of it, Zane talked him out of a box. We'd dip the ends of the pugil sticks in the blue chalk. That way, whenever you hit somebody, there was no chance of lying about whether you got speared or not. The blue spot on your shirt was enough to . . .

• • •

". . . thousand fifty-eight, thousand fifty-nine . . .

The sound of Chet's voice snapped me from my daydreams. As soon as I was alive again, I needed to take off before Daniel figured out where I was going. If I could find Foster . . . if I could talk him into voting for me . . .

". . . thousand *sixty*!"

I opened both eyes and sat up.

Foster Foster leaned down next to me. He reached out a hand and picked his pugil stick spear off the ground. It was the one that came flying at me from the pile of brush.

"Thanks for the new spear, Daniel," he called over his shoulder. "It's great. I'm going to have to throw it a few more times before I get accurate with it. I should have had Kent with that throw. But it's really neat."

Daniel shrugged. "Don't mention it. Soon as I get a little more money saved up from my allowance, I'm going to buy sticks for Kent and Jordan and Ted, too."

When I saw how proudly Foster held his new pugil stick, my heart sank.

Daniel Shift beat me to him. He bribed Foster with his very own pugil stick spear.

"It's just not fair," I mumbled.

"Oh, quit complaining." Daniel laughed. "It was a good ambush."

I wasn't even talking about that, but I couldn't say anything. Leading Daniel's horse, Zane rode up on his dapple gray mare and handed him the reins. "Where to now, General Swift?" He stuck his hand to the brim of his baseball cap like a salute.

"General?" I asked.

When Daniel stuck his nose in the air, it made him look like he had even less chin than normal.

"Yep. General."

My shoulders sagged. "I thought we were going to vote."

"We did. Chet, Pepper, Zane, and Foster all voted for me as general."

"But—"

"That's a majority," Daniel interrupted. "Even if Jordan and Ted vote for you, that still puts me one vote ahead. I'm making you captain, though. After Chet, you're next in command."

I stood there with my mouth open. Daniel put his foot in the stirrup, bounced once, and swung to the saddle.

"Troop, mount up!" he ordered. "We have to ride by Ted's and get him. Then we'll pick teams and have a real war before lunch."

Duke and I rode at the back of the line.

Captain Kent Morgan. It was almost enough to make me sick. Here I had dreams of being general of the Seventh Cavalry, and without even getting to vote, I'd been demoted to captain.

Bummer.

3

We rode across Wilson's Swamp, alongside Sinkhole River and headed up Bobcat Canyon.

Okay . . . Wilson's Swamp wasn't really a swamp. It was just sort of a muddy spot where one of the creeks flowed into Monster Lake—I mean, Cedar Lake. Right now it was all dried up because we hadn't had a rain since early June. Sinkhole River was really a little dried-up creek. We called it "Sinkhole" because there were a couple of deep pools that still had slimy, oozie green water in them. And "river" just sounded a lot more exciting than "creek."

We really did see a bobcat in Bobcat Canyon, though. It was about two years ago. He was a scrawny little thing. We thought he was somebody's house cat at first. But he was a real honest-to-goodness bobcat.

We almost didn't see him at all. That's because Zane was the one who spotted him. Usually, nobody ever listened to Zane. He was all the time making up stories or seeing stuff. If Pepper hadn't noticed the bobcat, right after Zane did—well . . .

We were near the head of Bobcat Canyon, where we saw the "real" bobcat, when we found Ted.

I guess I should say, Ted found us.

General Daniel Shift, our fearless leader, was in front of the line. I brought up the rear. With Chet close on his heels, Daniel kicked his horse and started up the steep path. He was almost to the top of the cliff when Ted Aikman sprang from behind a fallen oak log and drilled him—square in the chest—with a sunflower-stalk spear.

Startled, and probably a little hurt, Daniel grabbed his chest. Quick as a cat, Ted sprang to the side and launched another spear at Chet. It caught him totally by surprise, but Ted missed. Chet hopped off his horse and used him for a shield.

That's when the idea struck me. Why wait to choose teams, like General Swift suggested earlier. We all knew that Daniel, Chet, Pepper, and Zane would be on one team. Ted, Jordan, Foster, and I would be on the other. That's the way it always worked. So . . .

Nudging Duke with my heels, we trotted up beside Jordan. For once he was paying attention. I slipped my rubber knife from the scabbard at my side and nodded toward Pepper and Zane.

Jordan winked.

"Let's get 'em," he whispered.

Pepper never saw us coming. Jordan kicked his feet free from the stirrups and tucked them up on the saddle, under him. Pepper's horse didn't even shy when Jordan leaped from Mac and landed on his back.

Now, Jordan was kind of in a different world, most of the time. He was, however, smart enough to know that you don't drag Pepper Hamilton off his horse. Pepper outweighed any two or three of us put together. The chance of him landing on top of someone was simply too great a risk. So instead of trying to pull him off, Jordan just reached around and stabbed him in the chest.

Pepper did manage to yell out, though.

It was too late for Zane. Duke and I squeezed past Foster on the trail. We were right beside Zane when he looked up. His eyes flashed, just in time to see my blade coming toward his stomach. He sucked in, but it was no use. I got him.

His shoulders sagged and he sneered at me before he slumped in the saddle, then slid off Gray's back. When he yelled out, too, the element of surprise was lost.

I didn't even give Foster a second thought, since

he always ended up on our team. I guess his new "gift" from Daniel made him forget. He grabbed the pugil stick spear from where it rested across the front of his saddle, and jumped off his horse. He looked at me, then at Jordan, then back at me again.

Chet was closer. I turned my attention to him. Chet raised his head over the dip in his saddle. He ducked down, quick as he could. When a spear didn't come flying, he raised up again.

Still near the fallen log at the top of the cliff, Ted only had two sunflower stalks left. He wasn't about to waste one on a guy hiding behind a horse. Pugil stick spear in hand, and using his horse as a shield, Chet started toward me. Ted raised one of his spears, but Chet knew it was just a bluff.

"Jordan," I called. "Hurry up. I'm outnumbered."

Kneeling, I reached for Zane's spear. But he held on to it. I tugged. "You're dead. Let go."

"It's a 'death grip,'" he explained, still hanging on like a bulldog. "You'll have to pry my fingers loose."

My eyes crossed when I looked down my nose at him. I reached for his fingers, then gave it up. Chet was too close. There was no time.

"Jordan. Hurry!"

Slicing the air with my knife, I fended off Chet's first spear attack. He backed up, moving to the side for another try. That put Foster behind me. It was hard to watch Chet and wonder if Foster was sneaking up to stab me in the back.

"I got Foster," Jordan called. "Run from Chet, if you have to. Soon as I finish this guy off, I'll come help you."

It was mighty brave talk for Jordan. He wasn't that good at hand-to-hand combat. Usually—even if he was thinking about what he was doing—he ended up tripping over his feet or leaving himself wide open.

There was a sudden crashing sound behind me. Chet's mouth fell open and his spear dangled at his side. I glanced over my shoulder to see what was going on.

Tumbling and rolling like a bowling ball, Ted Aikman came from the top of the dirt cliff. Foster blinked. Then his eyes got as big around as baseballs. Ted was headed right for him.

Foster kind of hopped from one foot to the other—trying to decide which way to dodge. It was all Jordan needed. I guess he'd grabbed Pepper's spear, after he stabbed him. Jordan aimed it at Foster. Jabbed him in the side. The thing hit him so solid that a small cloud of blue chalk dust swirled through the air.

Foster didn't care that he'd been stabbed. He just wanted out of Ted's way. Ted wasn't rolling anymore. He was sliding. At least, I guess he was. I really couldn't tell. All I could see was this cloud of dust, rushing down the hill like an avalanche.

Foster started to jump left. He started to jump to the right. Only he couldn't decide. By the time he did . . .

It was too late.

Ted slammed into him. There was a yell—really more like a scream—then Foster's spear went flying. The next thing I saw were his tennis shoes. In the blink of an eye his feet were up above his head. Finally he disappeared into the cloud of rolling dust.

When the dirt settled, Ted appeared under Zane's horse's belly. Blinking and eyes still rolling, he staggered to his feet. The horse didn't kick or anything. He just wobbled his ears. Dizzy from rolling down the hill, Ted's eyes kind of jerked and twitched a moment before he found Chet. He fumbled for his knife.

The two of us started for the last enemy. Jordan was no help. All he did was laugh. Leaning against Zane's horse, he pointed at Foster, then at Ted, then back at Foster. He laughed so hard that water started leaking from his eyes.

"You—" He broke off, almost howling. "You should have seen . . . the look on . . . on Foster's face." Jordan finally managed. Then he dropped to his knees and wrapped his arms around the horse's hind leg.

All Ted, Chet, and I could do was shake our heads. Ted and I moved in for the kill. We came at Chet from opposite sides. Eased closer and closer, twisting our knives and watching his every move.

Chet dropped his spear. Both hands shot over his head. "I give! I surrender. You win."

The only difference between surrendering and getting killed was—if you were killed you had to lay quiet on the ground for sixty seconds. If you surrendered, you could at least stay on your feet and talk some. Chet knew he lost, and there was no sense getting all dirty.

I picked his spear up and turned to Ted.

"I'll watch the prisoner. You go get Jordan off the horse's leg, before he gets kicked in the head."

We probably had the best horses in the whole country. They weren't much good for racing or roping or anything like that, but when it came to fighting wars . . . our horses couldn't be beat.

Two years of jumping out of trees and knocking

people off their backs—two years of leaping from one horse onto another while galloping across a field—two years of getting hit with spears or sunflower stalks and having your rider fall off . . . the whole bunch of them had gotten used to just about anything.

Ted unwrapped Jordan's arms from around the hind leg and brought him over to where Chet and I stood.

Daniel got up and started dusting his jeans off. "That's cheating. Kent and Jordan were riding with us."

Jordan quit laughing just long enough to suck in a deep breath. "Kent and I weren't really on your team, Daniel. We were spies for Ted's team." With that, he looked back at Foster and burst out laughing again. The drops of water that leaked from his eyes left little mud trails down his cheeks.

I smiled, amazed at how sharp Jordan could be sometimes. Daniel folded his arms.

"It's not fair," he grumped.

"You're dead." I smiled at him. "Shut up or I'll kill you again."

Grudgingly, Daniel plopped down on his bottom and pouted.

"Thousand one," Ted began. "Thousand two . . . thousand three . . ."

"I'm tired of this war stuff." Daniel cupped his hands under what little chin he had, and stared at the dirt. "Let's go do something else."

Ted threw his hands up. "Now I got to start all over again."

I nudged him with my elbow. "I'll count. Thousand one . . . . thousand two . . . . thousand three . . . ."

4

Okay . . . so I overdid it on the counting. Trying to make it as slow and painful as possible . . . well, I took so long that even Ted and Jordan got a little ticked at me.

Besides, playing war was about all we had done for the three weeks that school had been out. It *was* getting kind of old. So when Pepper announced (at "a thousand twenty-eight") that his mom was making a batch of chocolate chip cookies when he left the house this morning—the war was over.

Dead guys leaped to their feet and ran for their horses. Even Jordan quit laughing long enough to wipe the mud streaks from his cheeks. I was ready to quit, too. I didn't even try to make Daniel lay back down.

"We can eat at my house and swim," Chet called. "I'll have Mrs. Garcia make some sandwiches."

The whole bunch of us charged off.

Jordan followed me south, back down Bobcat Canyon, alongside Sinkhole River, and across

Wilson's Swamp. Ted rode west to his farm and the rest of the guys headed north.

Jordan and I lived in South Shore Estates. There were ten twenty-acre lots on the south side of Cedar Lake—five lake-front and five lots across the road and up the hill. We lived in the very first house, right on the lake. Jordan and his family were next door. West of their house were the Fergusons, then the Brocks. Across the road is where the McBrides and the Taylors lived. Both those couples were sort of old, but they were nice. The lot next to Mrs. Baum's place was still for sale, as were the three across the road.

Mom and Dad got our twenty-acre lot before anyone else knew that Mr. Gregg, the dairy farmer who used to own the land on this side of Cedar Lake, was dividing it up.

That's 'cause Dad fished Mrs. Gregg out of the lake.

For a long time, Mom and Dad had been wanting to move out of the city. Dad was a paramedic with the fire department. We did okay, but paramedics aren't what you'd call rich. About three years ago, on his day off, Dad and one of his buddies were fishing near the Point, when they saw this hay truck bouncing and careening down the hill. It went smack-dab into Cedar Lake. They raced over and Dad jumped out and got the old woman loose from the truck before it went completely under. Mr. Gregg came running down the hill. His wife was fine, but when the truck lost its brakes and ended up in the water, it scared both of them half to death.

The Greggs thought Dad was a regular hero. Dad thought he was just doing what anybody would do, especially since he was a paramedic. They wanted to give him something or do something for him to show their appreciation, but Dad wouldn't have it. So they kind of sneaked around behind his back and went to Mom.

Somehow Mrs. Gregg found out that Mom was completing her real-estate license. She didn't pass the test the first time she took it. But six months later she did. How Mrs. Gregg knew, nobody could figure. But the day Mom passed her real-estate exam, Mrs. Gregg called and told her that they were retiring from the dairy business and were going to divide up their farm and sell it. She asked Mom to handle all the details and stuff that needed done. In return for her services, she would give us our choice of lots.

Now Mom was doing pretty well with her real estate sales. But back then we could never have afforded a place on Cedar Lake.

• • •

I put Duke's saddle and bridle in the shed, turned him into the pen, and gave him a helping of oats and sweet feed. Then I asked Mom if I could go swimming at Chet's, wrapped my bathing trunks in a towel, got my bicycle, and waited for Jordan.

And waited for Jordan . . .

And waited for Jordan . . .

After about twenty minutes I went after him. Mrs. Parks opened the door. She looked at me and gave kind of a helpless sigh.

"He was supposed to meet you, right?"

"Yes, ma'am."

Her shoulders sagged. She motioned toward Jordan's room. "He's on the computer."

Before I even opened the door to his room, I sucked in a deep breath.

"JORDAN!" I screamed as I burst through the doorway.

Startled, he looked up. "It might work." He smiled over at me and shoved his glasses up. "As many times as our dads have cut the line with their lawn mowers, we'd have to run it through PVC pipe, though. Otherwise, the moisture would short it out."

I must have looked like a total idiot. My mouth fell open so wide, a bird could have flown in and built a nest. My plan had been to startle *him*. Instead . . .

"What in the world . . ." I gasped.

"The telegraph cable." He shrugged. "If we bury the thing, it might work."

The guys had finished their sandwiches and cookies and were already in the pool by the time we got to Chet's.

Mrs. Garcia, the Bentlys' housekeeper, left a couple of sandwiches and some chips on the poolside table. I didn't eat mine. Instead I went for the chocolate chip cookies.

Guess I couldn't help myself. Pepper's mom and dad were rather large people—like Pepper. Mrs. Hamilton was about the same height as my mom, only she was kind of round. Mr. Hamilton was about six feet five. Every so often our families got together at their house for neighborhood cookouts and stuff. Next to our dads, Mr. Hamilton looked like a giant. Both of Pepper's parents were fantastic cooks. Pepper couldn't help being big.

The cookies were delicious.

After we swam for a while, the diving competition started. We really didn't choose sides, but all Daniel's guys gave his team good scores. And my guys—even when I tried to do a flip and ended up doing a belly-buster, gave me a 4.6.

Like I said, we didn't choose up teams, but . . .

When we got tired of diving and swimming, we dried off and got dressed.

The next day we chose up sides again and played bicycle polo. It was kind of like polo, only instead of using horses, we rode our bicycles. And instead of a wooden ball and mallets, we used a basketball and baseball bats.

The parking lot next to the boat ramp was our polo field—the outhouse was one goal and the "Permit Required" sign was the other. It was a fun game. We raced around on our bicycles, whacking that old basketball. Laughed, giggled, and had a regular blast, until . . .

Daniel's team got two goals behind. That's when it got serious. They tied the score, then Pepper crashed into the side of a pickup that some fisherman had parked there. It didn't leave much of a scratch. Even so, we headed for home as fast as we could go.

The next day we played football. Their team won. The day after that, we swam in Daniel's pool. We won the relay races. They won the diving competition. Today we did bicycle polo again.

We were lying around, resting, and just looking up at the sky when Daniel said: "Let's have another war, tomorrow." It sounded more like an order than a suggestion.

Jordan yawned. "I'm tired of playing war."

Nobody said anything. We just kind of grunted our agreement and kept watching the clouds.

"I got another idea," Daniel said. He sat up and looked straight at Ted. "Let's go fishing. We could choose up teams, and whoever comes in with the biggest and the most fish—"

"No!" Ted barked.

Mouths opened, the whole bunch of us sat up so quick it's a wonder we didn't pull a stomach muscle. Ted *always* wanted to go fishing. Ted loved fishing as much as Pepper loved eating. He lived and breathed for fishing. If someone so much as mentioned bait or worms or hooks, the smile on his face stretched clear up to his ears.

None of us could believe he was the one who yelled, "No!"

5

I thought you liked fishing," I said.

Ted sighed. "I do. I love to go fishing. But if it's going to be a competition . . . if we're gonna choose sides . . ." He sighed again, then took a deep breath as if he was trying to get himself back together or something.

"I love fishing," he repeated. "But I just want to go fishing. Have fun. We can't do *anything* without picking sides and trying to beat each other. We play war to see who wins. We play games like baseball and bicycle polo.

"I just want to catch fish—all of us—just to have fun. No contest. No game. Just fish. If we can't do that, I don't even want to go."

"Yeah," Jordan agreed. When he nodded, his glasses slipped. He had to shove them back up. "Ted's right. We're all the time having a contest. We can't even swim without making it a challenge. Remember how we judged the diving? We can't even play in the pool without trying to see who wins. Why don't we just go fishing like he said? We could maybe spend the night and cook out and . . ."

"Yeah." Zane leaped to his feet. "The lake monster only comes out at night. If we sleep out, maybe we can see it."

Like usual, we all ignored him.

"Our moms probably won't let us stay out all night, anyway," Chet grumped.

"Why not?" Daniel asked. "They wouldn't let us spend the night on the lake last year, but we're twelve, now. We're old enough. I bet we can talk them into it. And"—he smiled at Ted—"we don't have to see who catches the biggest or the most fish. We can just go together."

Ted smiled back. Zane gave a little wave with his arm, trying to get everyone's attention.

"The monster only comes out when there's a full moon. We can take turns standing guard. That way somebody's awake all the time and maybe we can spot him."

No one so much as looked up at Zane.

"We could cut bank poles and use shad gizzards," Ted suggested.

Daniel cocked his head to one side. "What are bank poles?"

"Well, they're just willow trees. You cut 'em down and sharpen one end and put a hook . . . and . . . well, I'll just have to show you."

"What are shad gizzards?" Foster wondered.

"Well, they're . . . ah . . . they're inside shad and ah . . . er . . . and . . . I got no idea."

"A gizzard is an internal organ in earthworms and birds. Also found in some fish, it aids in the digestion of food." When Jordan explained stuff, he sounded like an encyclopedia. "It's kind of hard and helps grind their food."

"Yeah," Ted agreed, pointing at Jordan. "What he said. It's kind of hard, so it stays on a fishing hook real well."

"Where do we get them?" I asked.

"Like, duh," Ted sneered at me. "You get them from shad."

I sneered right back and wobbled my head. "Like, duh. Where do we find the shad?"

"Oh." He gave a sheepish grin and ducked his head. "The shad feed in the shallows down under the dam. You know, where the water runs over? We'd have to take our bows and some real arrows and—"

Zane moaned. "I want to see the monster."

Daniel propped his elbow on his knee and rested his chin on his fist. Only with not much chin, it looked like he was resting his bottom lip on his fist.

"Would you knock it off. There *is* no lake monster."

"I swear," Zane protested. "I saw his eyes shining under the water. I really did."

"Two years ago you saw that mountain lion," Jordan said. "Thing was nothing but a scraggly old house cat."

"The year before that, you saw a black bear," Ted reminded him. "Only it turned out to be an Angus cow's rump."

"And when was it you saw Big Foot?" Chet asked.

Zane folded his legs and flopped down on the ground. He tipped over backward to stare up at the clouds. "I was just teasing about that Big Foot thing. I told you guys that."

Now that we had Zane shut up about the lake monster, we turned our attention back to the fishing trip.

"Do we need worms and minnows, too?" Chet asked.

"When can we get started?"

"We'll go tomorrow night." Ted was on his feet now. "That would give us time to get all the stuff ready. Everybody go home, check with your

parents—beg if you have to—then call my house.
Okay?"

Dad's pickup wasn't in the drive when I got home.
I put my bicycle away and went inside to see what
Mom was doing. She had just started supper.
Something sizzled in the pan on the stove. I eased
up beside her to see what we were having.

She smiled at me, then her nose kind of crinkled.
"What have you been doing?"

"Bicycle polo."

She leaned away from me, so far to one side that
I thought she was going to tip over. After I told her
about the game and how much fun we had, Mom
politely suggested that I go take a shower before
supper.

I heard Dad's pickup pull in while I was washing my hair. They were both at the table by the
time I got dried off and slipped into some clean
clothes.

When asking to spend the night out on the lake
with the guys—timing is critical. First off, I didn't
just march in and blurt it out. I sat down at the
table and listened for a while. If either of my parents was in a bad mood or had had trouble at
work, asking should be put off until after dinner.

Dad's shift at the fire department was pretty calm. He only had to work two car accidents and nobody was hurt. Mom thought the house she was trying to sell in town was pretty much a "done deal." So she was in a good mood, too.

Dad and I helped set the table while Mom finished up the fried okra and got the meat loaf out of the oven. Since both had had a good day, as soon as Dad finished saying grace, I would ask.

Before I could say anything, Mom folded her arms and rocked back in her chair. "I wish there was something we could do for Emma," she said. "I just feel so sorry for her."

"Money problems again?" Dad stopped his forkful of meat loaf just short of his lips.

Mom sighed and laced her fingers together. "Yeah. Between having her husband in that nursing home, and taxes, and trying to keep that old truck of hers going . . . I just don't see how she can make it much longer."

"What happened to her husband, anyway?"

"Had a massive stroke." Mom sighed. "Can't speak or walk. He can feed himself, but . . ." She stopped and shook her head. "I went with Emma to visit him at the nursing home one time. She goes every single day."

"You go up to her place, today?"

"Yes. She called just before three. Emma's thinking about selling part of the farm. I tried to tell her that if she divided the lakefront up into three lots, that would bring in a bunch more than the rest of the place all put together. She won't have it. She's bound and determined to keep all the land from the house down to the water."

Dad frowned. "She doesn't ski or swim or fish. Why does she need the lakefront?"

"No idea. She won't part with it, though. Emma refuses to sell anything between the house and the water."

"Who's Emma?" I interrupted.

Both had just stuffed some fried okra in their mouths. Mom held up a finger, asking me to wait a second. When she finished chewing, she dabbed the corners of her mouth with a napkin.

"Mrs. Baum," she answered.

I felt my eyes flash.

"That nasty old grouch who lives at the end of the road? You know her?"

Mom and Dad both stopped eating and glared at me.

"Emma Baum is one of the sweetest little ladies I ever met." Mom's eyes were tight. "I *never* want to hear you call her a nasty old grouch, or any such thing. Not ever again! Understand?"

"Yes, ma'am."

Okay—so maybe supper wasn't the right time to ask about going fishing. Maybe tomorrow would be better.

6

I'd learned, a long time ago, that when you screw up—big time—it's best to keep your mouth shut.

I sat quiet as a mouse through the rest of supper. They talked about how Mrs. Baum brought cookies and walked down to visit when they first moved in. And all the other nice things she had done since we moved here. Dad remembered how he lost his watch out in our hay barn, and she brought her metal detector to help him find it. Mom repeated about how she went to visit her husband every day in the nursing home and how hard she worked on her garden, behind her house. "She always shares tomatoes and okra—anything she takes from that garden."

The conversation finally left Mrs. Baum and went to money in the savings account and bills— all the stuff grown-ups usually talk about. I kept my mouth shut. When I helped with the dishes— I kept my mouth shut. And when I finally felt like they'd forgotten what I said and I was in the clear,

I headed off to my room. I'd just stay out of the way until the homemade ice cream was ready.

I had just turned on my computer when the phone rang.

"Kent, it's for you," Mom called.

Since they were in the living room, I picked up the phone in the kitchen.

"Everybody's called but you." Ted's voice was a little hard to hear. That's because our ice-cream maker made such a loud grinding noise.

"What?" I cupped my hand around the phone and turned away from the freezer.

"All the guys can go," Ted said. "They've already called. Why haven't you?"

I humped my shoulders, trying to shield the ear piece from the noise.

"I haven't asked them, yet," I confessed, glancing around to make sure they weren't in the room.

"Why not?"

"Well, I was going to. Only Mom mentioned something about Mrs. Baum, and I blurted out about what a nasty old grouch she was. I just can't stand that old witch. I wish she'd just . . ."

The words trickled from my mouth, then faded into complete silence when I caught the movement from the corner of my eye. Slowly I turned. Mom stood beside the door. Arms folded, she stared at me. I wished I could have caught the words and stuffed them back in my mouth. Instead, they hung over my head—floating about the kitchen like an ominous black cloud.

Screw up once—there's a good chance your parents will forgive and forget. If you screw up twice—you're gonna pay for it. Mom marched us and the nearly frozen homemade ice cream down to Mrs. Baum's.

"It's not fair!"

"Quit whining and keep walking," Dad growled. "We're parents. Parents don't have to be fair. Besides, it wasn't that bad, was it?"

Dad walked beside me, carrying the empty ice-cream freezer. A few steps ahead of us, Mom led the way down the road. She glanced over her shoulder.

"Didn't I tell you she was nice?" Mom smiled. "When you're afraid of something, it's usually because you don't know enough about it. Like me. I used to be afraid of snakes. My fourth-grade teacher had a boa constrictor. I studied and learned everything I could about snakes, and by the end of the year I could hold the thing. People are a lot the same way. Sometimes we don't like someone simply because we don't know them. I knew that if you got to know Mrs. Baum, you'd just love her."

I got to know Mrs. Baum, all right. I knew her a whole bunch better than I ever wanted to. I knew she was seventy-eight years old. I knew her husband was named Jeb. He used to be a miner. I knew he worked in mines all up and down the West Coast. I also knew that he had a stroke eight years ago, and they had to put him in the nursing home. I knew that it was really expensive to keep someone in a nursing home. And I knew she made good oatmeal cookies.

There were some other things I knew, too.

Only they weren't things I could mention to Mom and Dad. I knew that probably the only reason she was nice to me was because they were along. I bet if they hadn't been there, she'd have run me off with a broom or something.

And I knew she lied.

Mom had asked her why she didn't want people on her front pasture. The wrinkled old woman hesitated a moment, then kind of stammered when she started to explain.

"Well . . . my . . . ah . . . my husband and I spent some time looking for the jar of silver dollars my father buried." The way her eyes jumped around, and the way she wouldn't look us in the face—I could tell she wasn't being honest. "We also have lots of gophers. I'm sure you've noticed the mounds. Whenever we dug into a gopher run, Jeb would cover the hole with a piece of wood. Then instead of having to dig a new hole to put gopher poison in, all he had to do was lift the wood. A lot of the boards got covered with dirt and grass. I wouldn't want one of the horses to break a leg."

Mom thought it made sense. As far as I was concerned, Mrs. Baum just made it up—she was hiding something.

While I waited for Mom to open the front door, I patted my tummy. Still, I thought to myself, she sure makes good oatmeal cookies.

I felt like I'd just gotten to sleep when . . . WHOOOP!

Something clunked me on the head. My eyes flashed wide. The breath caught in my throat. Waving my arms to fend off whatever it was that attacked me, I sat straight up in bed and swung my legs over the side.

"What . . . who . . ." I stammered.

"Get up, you lazy nerd. We got to go shoot shad and cut bank poles."

"Who hit me? What's . . . what's going on?"

Ted stood beside my bed. Grinning like some kind of idiot, he held my pillow in both hands. He drew it back over his shoulder like he was getting ready to swing at me again.

I waved him off with my hands. Blinking a couple of times, I glanced at the window. A pale glow came through my blinds. It was morning, but the sun was barely up. "What are you doing in my room? I haven't even talked to my folks yet. Give me a second to wake up."

Ted tossed the pillow at me. I knocked it away. He laughed.

"Come on, sleepyhead. I've already asked them. They said okay. Get up. Get your clothes on. We got places to go. People to see. Things to do."

"What people?" I yawned.

"It's just an expression. Now get out of bed. Let's go." He headed for the door. "Oh, be sure and bring your bow," he called over his shoulder.

Ted was sitting on his bicycle, waiting for me. As soon as I walked out the front door, he took off. Holding my bow across the handlebars, I leaped on my bike and chased after him.

"You know anything about Mrs. Baum?" I asked after I caught up and got my breath.

Ted glanced over at me. "Not much. Her husband and my grandfather used to be pretty good friends. Did a lot of farming together and stuff.

She always seemed nice—unless you try to ride your horse across the front of her place."

"Yeah." I nodded. "Mom and Dad think she's nice, too. Only all she ever does is yell at Jordan and me. You know why she doesn't want people messing around on her place?"

Ted nodded. "It's on account of holes her husband dug and covered up with wood."

I shook my head. "How come you never told me that?"

Ted shrugged. "You never asked."

Mr. Aikman was working on his tractor when we got to Ted's farm. When he saw us ride up, he waved.

"Hang on a minute, boys," he called. "Let me get this bolt back in here, then I'll be ready."

We dropped our kickstands and sat down in the shade to wait.

"I sure hope we catch something tonight. This week and next are about all we have left of summer."

"What?" I yelped. "What do you mean, all we have left of summer? It's only the end of June."

Ted yawned, lay back on the grass, and just stared up at the clouds. "No, I mean the last time we'll have the whole bunch of us together. After the Fourth of July everybody takes off for vacations and church camp and stuff."

"Yeah," I agreed. "Jordan and his folks are leaving for Colorado. I think Foster's going to see relatives in South Carolina."

"Pepper, Chet, and Daniel are taking their vacation *together* this summer. Know where?" Ted asked.

"Where?"

"Well you know Samantha, Pepper's sister, is getting married."

"Yeah, I know."

"They're having a shower for her next Sunday."

"Okay. So?"

"So, Pepper's mom and dad asked her where she wanted to go on her honeymoon. When she told them, they all decided to go along and make a vacation out of it. Then all three families got to talking about it and decided to take their vacation together. They won't stay at the same place where Samantha and her new husband are staying. But guess where all three families are going."

I was getting just a little put out with Ted. It was too hot and too early in the morning to be playing guessing games.

"I don't really care."

But when Ted didn't say anything else, I asked anyway: "Where?"

"Hawaii."

"Hawaii?" I was suddenly wide awake and interested. "Man, I wish we could do that. I don't even think we're going to take a vacation this year."

"How come?"

"Dad has to get certified again in underwater rescue. Summer is the only time they offer the classes."

"You getting certified, too?"

I shook my head. "Can't. You have to be twelve to get certified in scuba. I can do that. But it's twenty-one for underwater rescue. He's taking me, anyway. I go through the training—just don't get the certificate. How about you?"

Ted sighed. "Not going anyplace, either. Just staying home and helping with the farm. That's all I ever do." He paused a minute and stared off at the blue sky. "Man, I hope we catch some fish tonight."

Truth of the matter was, I didn't care that much one way or the other. I mean . . . if we had to go fishing, catching something was better than just sitting around. What I really wanted was to go someplace exciting—like Hawaii. I wanted to do something fun and adventurous.

Fishing . . . well, fishing was just fishing. How exciting could that be?

7

When Mr. Aikman finished with his tractor he strolled over to join us.

"Don't have to shoot shad," he said. "Went by the bait shop for coffee this morning. They usually don't have shad gizzards. They did today. Got you three cartons of them."

"How about cut bait?" Ted asked.

"Catch some perch down at the lake. Let's go get the poles done first."

Ted and I nodded and followed Mr. Aikman to his pickup. I guess I was a little disappointed. Using the bow and arrow to shoot at fish sounded like it might have been fun. Still—chopping down trees might be neat, too.

We bounced and jostled across the pasture, to a little creek at the far side of Ted's farm. Mr. Aikman hopped out and grabbed his chain saw. He found some willow trees and started cutting them, right at the base. Ted told me that was to keep the little stumps from puncturing a tractor tire if he drove down here.

He cut about twenty trees. All of them were eight to ten feet long and pretty straight. All Ted and I had to do was take an ax or hatchet from the back of the truck and knock the limbs off so we had a pole. He said he'd come back and check on us in a couple of hours.

I never sweated so much in my life.

It was three hours before Mr. Aikman came back, and we were just finishing up.

Only, we weren't finished.

He took an ax and chopped at the base of one of the poles. He whacked and sliced until that end was sharpened to a point. Then, with a smile, he handed the ax to Ted.

"Check on you again, in about an hour."

So Ted and I chopped and sweated some more.

When we were done, we had about twenty bank poles. Mr. Aikman helped us load them in the back of his truck. As we bounced across the pasture, he took his cap off and started fanning it at us.

"What?" Ted asked finally.

"You two boys really been working hard," Mr. Aikman teased. "Just trying to keep the air moving the *other* direction."

Feeling a little self-conscious, I kind of leaned away.

"We're just going fishing," Ted teased back. "You think we need to take a bubble bath before we go?"

"You're fine," his dad chuckled. "Don't bother cleaning up. If I were you, after we stick the bank poles in the mud, I'd just stay there in the water and let the odor ooze out. Every catfish in the lake will swim over to see what died." He clamped his lips together.

Ted stuck his tongue out. He was sitting shotgun. Since he was on the other side of me, I guess he figured his dad couldn't see. But all at once Mr. Aikman's eyebrows arched.

"Watch it. You stick that thing out again, I'll reach over and tie a knot in it." He tried to sound serious, but I could tell he wasn't. Dad and I had fun teasing each other like that. It was neat listening to Ted and his dad go at it.

At the house Mr. Aikman got some nylon fishing line and hooks from his tackle box. We tied the line at the very tip of the poles. Then Mr. Aikman stretched it out, cut it at the right length, and helped us tie on the hooks. He told Ted to go inside and take a shower. We put my bicycle in the back, and he drove me home.

"I'll give you and Ted time to get your fishing gear and grab a bite to eat. Then we'll go set the poles out and catch some perch for cut bait."

"How big do they need to be?" I asked.

"Doesn't matter. Anything you catch is a keeper. All we're going to do is slice them into strips and put them on the hooks."

"Should we get some ice out of the freezer to keep them fresh?"

Mr. Aikman smiled and shook his head. "Don't want 'em fresh. The more they stink, the better catfish like 'em."

At the house I got my fishing gear out of the garage so it would be ready when Ted and Mr. Aikman came back for me. Then I tossed my sweaty shirt and jeans into the washing machine. I took a nice hot bath instead of a shower. That's because my arm was kind of stiff and hurting from all the chopping we did. I was so tired, all I wanted to do was plop down in front of the TV and go to sleep. I hadn't even gotten my soccer shorts on when the phone rang.

"Kent. It's for you," Mom called from her office.

I trotted to the kitchen and grabbed the phone. "Hello."

"Kent? This is Jordan. I asked my father where he thought we should fish tonight. He informed me that if we were going for bass or crappie, we should probably fish off the Point. He also related the fact that catfish feed where the wind and currents agitate the bottom. Consequently, this side of the lake would be advantageous for catfish. Daniel wants to bring the horses so we can ride around the lake tomorrow morning. Foster says they'll just be in the way. What's your opinion?"

I held the phone out at arm's length and stared at it. Why did Jordan always have to use such big words and make stuff sound like a dictionary?

"I don't know." I sighed. "What did Ted say?"

"I'll call him. Call you back."

I had just turned the TV on and plopped on the couch when the phone rang again. For the next forty-five minutes I felt as if my cheeks had springs in them. Every time they touched the couch, I bounced back up and ran for the phone.

About the time Ted and his dad showed up, we finally decided to go on our side of the lake and bring the horses.

Spending the night in my own front yard didn't sound all that exciting. So I asked Mom if it would be okay to camp on the vacant lot between the Brocks' and Mrs. Baum's place. She said it would be fine—just so long as we didn't leave paper and trash all over.

• • •

Ted put his horse in our pen with Duke, while his dad drove the bank poles down to the lake. Foster put his horse in Jordan's lot with Mac. Daniel's guys had leather hobbles for their horses. They put them in the vacant lot near where we pitched Ted's and Daniel's tents.

We made camp near a little creek, about thirty feet up the hill from the lake. Where we were— well . . . even if we stayed up all night, making racket, we were far enough from any houses that the noise wouldn't bother people.

Mr. Aikman had changed out of his farming clothes and into his bathing suit. When Mr. Bently brought the ice chests in the back of his SUV, he had his suit on, too. While we unloaded the food and worked on the tents, they started setting out the bank poles.

And—with two dads and eight boys, all working together, we had our camp set up in less than thirty minutes. Mr. Aikman and Mr. Bently made sure we had plenty of rocks around our fire area to make it safe, then they wished us luck and told us if there were any problems to go to Jordan's house. It was the closest. We grabbed our fishing rods and started putting hooks or plugs on.

"Where's the boat?" Foster asked.

Ted frowned at him. "What boat?"

"To paddle out and put the bait on the bank poles."

"We don't have a boat. No sense in worrying about bank poles now. We'll bait 'em up right before dark."

"But how are we going to put the bait on them without a boat?" Jordan asked.

Ted's frown curled to a sly smile. "We just wade out and put it on."

"But none of us brought a bathing suit," Pepper protested.

"So?" Ted shrugged.

Mouths gaping open, the whole bunch of us turned to glare at him.

"You mean . . ."

Ted nodded. "After dark nobody can see us. We're not close to anyone's house. And we're just a bunch of guys. Who needs a bathing suit?"

8

The thought of wading around, shoulder deep in a lake . . . in the dark . . . without a stitch of clothes on except for our tennis shoes . . . well . . . There could be all sorts of stuff swimming in that water . . . and at night . . . when we couldn't see . . . with nothing on . . .

I don't guess any of us were that excited about the idea.

So we fished from the bank and never gave it another thought—until it started getting dark.

Jordan and I offered to run home and get our bathing trunks. Zane asked if we had enough suits for everyone.

"Nobody can see us," Ted scoffed. "You guys aren't sissies, are you?"

That shut us up. We each dug into the big ice chest and grabbed another pop, then sat down around the little fire that Mr. Bently started for us before he left. Pepper guzzled another Coke, then grabbed a handful of chocolate chip cookies.

"Where's the bathroom?" he asked, wiping his

chin. "Do we walk up to Jordan's house?"

Ted slammed the lid shut on his tackle box. "Haven't you guys ever camped out before? You don't go barging into somebody's house." He reached into one of the paper sacks and tossed Pepper a roll of toilet paper. "Here. Go down to the creek."

Pepper tossed the roll back to him. "I don't need that. Just gotta pee."

"Then go anyplace." Zane chuckled. "But not near the tents."

"Yeah," Ted added. "Not on the fire, either. Makes the hot dogs taste funny."

Pepper sneered at both of them and trotted off toward the trees that lined the creek.

"We need to start out with a variety of bait," Ted explained. "We'll put cut bait on the first hook, minnows on the second, worms on the third, and shad gizzards on the fourth. Then we'll start over again till we have all the lines baited. We have to check the hooks about once an hour, see what they're hitting, and put on fresh bait. Who's going with me?"

Nobody looked up. We just sat there, drinking our pops and staring at the fire.

"Come on, guys." Ted moaned. "It's not like you have to go every time. We take turns. Two guys bait the hooks. An hour later the next two guys go take the fish off and put fresh bait on." He paused. Still no one would look at him. "I'll go twice. No, three times. But somebody's got to go with me. I can't carry the bait and take fish off all by myself."

The fire was really interesting. I guess it was downright hypnotizing, the way everybody just sat, trance-like, and stared at it. The flames all orange, and red, and yellow, and blue. The coals . . . glowing and shimmering, almost as if they were alive . . .

"Come on, guys. You're acting like a bunch of wimps."

Maybe we needed to add a little more wood and a log or two. Let the logs burn down to coals, and it would be just right for cooking hot dogs and . . .

"All right! I'll just pick somebody."

I cringed. So did everybody else.

"Kent."

My shoulders sagged so far that my elbows nearly bumped the ground. I liked having Ted as my best friend. It did have its drawbacks, though. I set my pop down and slowly got to my feet. Ted stripped off his shirt, then unsnapped his jeans. I did the same. He kicked his pants off. I did the same. He peeled his socks off. I did the same. Then . . .

I smiled when he stuffed his feet back into his

tennis shoes. He left his jockey shorts on! Maybe this wasn't going to be so bad, after all.

"You get the can of shad gizzards and the worms. I'll get the cut bait and the minnows."

Ted grabbed two pieces of rope and tossed one to me. He took one of the cans of shad gizzards, and handed me a white Styrofoam carton of worms. I didn't even have a chance to ask him what the rope was for, when he snatched up the tin can where we had put the cut-up perch and headed for the lake.

My minnow bucket shell sat in the edge of the water. The outside part—the shell—was like a round, tin bucket with a bail or handle. The inside part of the minnow bucket—the part with all the holes—fit or slid down inside the shell. It had the lid and a Styrofoam thing under the edge to keep it afloat. When we first got here, we took the inside part out, attached it with our metal stringer to the shell, and tossed it into the lake. All the little holes on the inside part let the water flow through. That way the minnows could breathe. It kept them alive a lot longer than if we just left it in the shell on the bank.

I glanced down, making sure there was plenty of water inside the shell. Water kept the thing weighted down so the part with the holes and minnows wouldn't float away. Pepper and Chet brought their minnow buckets, too. All three were sitting in a row on the bank. The insides—the part with all the holes—glided and bobbed around in the shallows.

Ted grabbed hold of the metal stringer on the handle of my bucket. He unsnapped it from the bail and hooked it on to the rope around his waist.

I tied my rope around my waist. Ted handed me the tin can with the cut bait. Then . . .

Ted stripped his jockey shorts off.

I just stood there. Ted strolled a little ways into the lake. When I didn't follow, he paused and glanced back at me.

"I . . . I thought we were going to . . . ah . . . leave our . . . ah . . ." I stammered.

Ted shrugged. "You know what wet underpants feel like? There's no way I'm sitting around, all night, in soggy shorts. Come on."

I had a carton of worms in one hand and a tin can full of cut-up perch in the other. Slowly I put them on the ground. Mustering all my courage, I stuck my thumbs under the elastic and peeled them down.

Behind me—up the hill—somebody whistled.

"Look!" one of the other guys yelled. "Must be a little bunny rabbit down by the lake. All I can see is its shiny white cottontail."

Then somebody else started singing "Here

Comes Peter Cottontail." Before I knew it, the whole bunch joined in on the song.

I felt like a total idiot.

Here I was with the cold, dark, murky lake on one side. And on the other side all the guys whistling catcalls and singing a song I hadn't heard since second grade.

Tin can full of cut bait in one hand and a Styrofoam carton of worms in the other, I took a deep breath and tromped out into the lake.

The water was a lot colder than I expected. I stayed on my tiptoes for as long as I could, but it was no use.

Chest deep in the cold lake, Ted waited at the first bank pole with a disgusted look on his face until I caught up with him.

"Told you it wasn't that bad." He smiled and tried to hand me his can of shad gizzards. "Here, hold this while I put the cut bait on the hook."

"What am I supposed to hold it with—my teeth?"

Ted looked at the carton of worms and the tin can I was holding.

"Got a point." He shrugged. "When we get back to the bank, we're gonna have to reorganize. Next trip out, it'll be dark and someone will have to carry a flashlight."

Holding the tin can full of shad gizzards under his chin, Ted grabbed hold of the string that dangled from the tip of the bankpole. When he did, he almost lost the can. He had to catch it, then hump his shoulder forward to trap the can between his shoulder and jaw.

"Ad's ot da string ong enough so it dangles oose on the ottom."

"What?" I frowned.

Ted let go of the string and took the can from between his shoulder and chin.

"I said, 'Dad's got the string long enough so it dangles loose on the bottom.'"

I rolled my eyes. Ted sighed and stuck the can back under his chin.

"'At way e atfish can et it all in eir outh."

"Huh!"

He glanced up at me and moved the can once more. "That way the catfish can get it all in their mouths. When they try to swim off, they end up hooking themselves."

He started to stick the can back against his shoulder, then stopped. "You ever help your mom carry glasses or drinks to the table?"

"Sure." I answered.

"Okay," he said with a grin. "Hold the worms with the thumb and first finger of your left hand.

Now hold the cut bait with the thumb and finger of your right hand. See? Got six fingers left over. Here. Hold the shad gizzards."

Ted threaded the cut bait onto the hook, then sloshed on toward the next pole. Following him, I felt like a circus clown trying to juggle stuff. It was hard to hold all three containers. If I tripped over a submerged branch or so much as slipped in the mud, I'd drop the whole thing. Most of our bait would be gone. Nothing more than a free meal for some fish.

But that wasn't the worst part.

When boys are skinny-dipping—especially in the dark—there are certain parts of our bodies that we like to protect. Well . . . maybe not *like* to . . . maybe it's more we *feel* like we *need* to protect. I mean, there could be fish or snakes or turtles down there and . . .

Anyway, with the Styrofoam carton of worms in one hand and the tin can full of cut bait in the other, with the shad gizzards trapped between—my hands were pretty well tied up. Sloshing around made me really nervous. It was a creepy feeling . . . like I needed to at least wave my hand around—to chase away anything that might be too close.

"I got an idea," I said when we reached the next bank pole.

"What?"

"Why don't we pour the shad gizzards in with the cut bait?"

Ted frowned, thinking about it for a moment. "Good idea. When we come back out to check for fish, we're gonna need a flashlight. That way, one guy's got a free hand to hold the light, while the other's getting the fish off. Smart thinking, Kent."

He took three minnows out of his bucket and threaded them on to the hook on the second pole. After he let the line go so it would sink back to the bottom, he took the tin can from between my fingers. He didn't dump it into the cut bait can. Instead, he poured the shad gizzards into his minnow bucket. Sure they were all out, he filled the can with water and let it sink.

We weren't supposed to litter. But there was no way I was going to dive down and try to retrieve that can. I was just glad to have it out of my hands so I could "protect" myself while we waded to the third bank pole.

Having at least one hand free to wave around down there from time to time . . . well, it just made me feel a lot more secure. Ted was right. It really wasn't so bad, after all.

Then again . . . coming back out here . . . when it was really dark . . . holding a flashlight . . .

9

The rest of the guys had already started cooking hot dogs by the time we put the bait up, pulled on our underwear, and walked back to the campsite. Ted and I put our jeans on but didn't bother with our shirts. After being in the cool lake, the warm evening breeze felt pretty good.

Jordan handed me a clothes hanger. "It's almost done." He nodded toward the frank on the end. "Depends on how you like your hot dog."

I squatted down beside the fire. Daniel came up and sat next to me. Pepper sat across from us. He had three wieners on his coat hanger. The thing was so heavy he couldn't keep them out of the ashes. I found a place where the coals glowed almost white hot and held my hot dog just above them. Daniel scooted closer. I couldn't help but notice that he held his coat hanger so high above the coals that the thing wouldn't even get warm, much less cook.

One at a time the guys drifted off to put mustard or chili and pickle relish on their buns. When there were just the two of us left beside the fire, Daniel scooted even closer. He kind of looked around, making sure no one was listening.

"Was it scary?" he whispered. "I mean . . . you know . . . out there with nothing on and . . . dark . . . and, well, you know?"

I did what any normal, red-blooded male would do.

I lied.

Before we were finished eating supper, every single one of the guys managed to catch me alone and ask the very same thing.

"Nothing to it," I boasted. "No, it wasn't scary at all. I mean, nothing's going to bother you. It was kind of fun—honest."

We chowed down until everyone was totally stuffed, added wood to the fire so it wouldn't go out, and decided to fix the s'mores *after* we fished for a while.

Our tackle boxes, rods and reels, along with the bait were already down at the lake. We took flashlights and put weights on our lines so we could throw them out farther.

"Before we start fishing, we need to check the bank poles again," Ted called out. "I don't want to go sloshing around with all your hooks and lines in the water. If I bump somebody's pole, one of you idiots might think you have a fish. You'd yank and I'd end up with a hook in my leg. Come on, Kent."

I put my rod down and started to get up.

"I'll go with you." Daniel hopped to his feet. "I'm not scared."

When they stripped, there was another chorus of "Here Comes Peter Cottontail." None of the bank poles had been touched, so it took Ted and Daniel hardly any time at all to run them. Still, Daniel gave me sort of a funny look when they got back. They put their pants on, and we all shined our flashlights out onto the lake. Once we had the bank poles spotted, we cast our lines, trying to get between them so we wouldn't get hung up.

We sat there for a long time, talking about school, and where we would like to go on vacation, and which girls we thought were cute and which were nice, and telling ghost stories. But when Foster pulled in a two-pound catfish and then Chet caught one that weighed a pound and a half, there were suddenly more important things to do than talk.

Over the next two hours or so, we ended up catching fourteen fish with rods and reels, and nineteen more off the bank poles. About midnight, when things started to slow, we began wandering back up the hill.

We stuffed ourselves with s'mores. Aside from an occasional sword fight with the coat hangers— trying to knock the other guy's marshmallows off or get them all covered with ashes—making s'mores was pretty uneventful. When we were so full we could hardly stand the thought of sticking another marshmallow over the flames, we all got our sleeping bags and made a circle around the campfire.

Pepper started snoring the second his back hit the sleeping bag. Some of the guys visited. Others—like me—stretched out for a short nap.

I barely got my eyes closed when Ted nudged me with his foot.

"It's our turn on the bank poles."

I yawned and looked up at him. "You sure? What time is it?"

"Fifteen till one."

"Let's get some sleep."

Ted glanced around, then leaned close to my ear. "Lots of times the big fish come up after the little ones have fed," he whispered. "Come on."

The first five bank poles hadn't been touched. But when Ted started pulling up the line on pole number six, he suddenly let go and jumped back.

"What?" I gasped.

"Fish." He breathed. "Big one, too." He pulled up the stringer that was attached to his rope and had me shine the light on it. It was almost full. "Wait here," he said. "We're gonna need a fresh stringer for this guy. He's big. I don't want to lose him."

Walking around, with nothing on, in a dark lake wasn't my idea of fun. Course, after three trips to check the bank poles, I'd almost gotten used to it. But standing there . . . all alone . . . in the dark . . . the quiet . . .

It took forever for Ted to get back.

"I'm gonna need both hands," he said, motioning me toward the bank pole. "You'll have to hold the light and bring the fish up—real slow. Don't yank on him. He's gonna jerk and flop around, but just keep pulling slow and steady." He opened the wire hook at the end of the stringer, then checked to make sure the other end was secured to the rope around his waist. "Don't lift him out of the water, though. Soon as I see him, I'll ram the stringer through his bottom lip. Don't even think about letting go of the line until I got the stringer latched. Okay?"

"Okay."

Holding the flashlight in one hand, I used the

other to get hold and start lifting the line. A sudden tug yanked the nylon cord from my fingers. I reached down and got a better grip.

Again a strong, solid jerk pulled the line from my grasp. A chill raced up my back. Ted wasn't kidding. This guy *was* big. The anticipation tingled up my spine and pounded inside my head. I stuck the flashlight handle back in my mouth, tilted sideways so the light was on the string, and grabbed the line with both hands.

The instant the fish's broad, flat mouth broke the surface, Ted jabbed the stringer through his bottom lip. How he managed to latch it, I still don't know.

The spray that came when the fish lurched and tried to take off shot water high into the air. It got my eyes, face, hair. The nylon cord dug into my fingers. My jaws locked. My teeth ground together, I was so determined not to let him go.

"Got him," Ted whispered. I worked my hands loose and wiped the water from my eyes. Taking the light out of my mouth, I shined it on my hands. There were red marks where the line had dug in, but they weren't bleeding. Ted raised the stringer so we could see our trophy. The fish was still long enough that its back half was underwater.

"He'll go fifteen pounds." Ted panted. "Maybe twenty or more."

"Let's go show the guys."

Ted shushed me. "No. Let's see what else we got on the bank poles. Can you imagine how they'd flip out if we came back with ten of these things on our stringer?"

Even though Ted's rope belt was tied tight around his waist, and even though the stringer was secure, he still kept checking it. About three poles farther, we caught another fish. This one was smaller, but still a lot larger than the channel cat we caught on rods and reels.

Right in the middle of our bank pole line—the place where we were closest to the campsite—we slowed our pace. We didn't talk or slosh as we moved through the water. It was as if we had given some unspoken signal that we'd do nothing to tip the guys off about the fantastic catch we had. We wouldn't even let them know we were around until we had more fish to show off when we got back beside the light of the fire. And we would . . .

All of a sudden something wet . . . and slimy . . . and cold . . . touched me . . . in a place where I *didn't* want to be touched!

Eyes flashed. Fists and hands slammed into the

water, fending off whatever it was that attacked me. I ran for the bank.

Someone yelled. I think it was me. To be honest, it sounded more like a scream, but I don't remember screaming or yelling, either one. When I glanced back, something was there.

Eyes!

Glowing, yellow eyes stared at me. Running harder, I opened my mouth. Not a single sound came out.

Then somebody else screamed.

I glanced over the other shoulder. There were no eyes, but Ted was charging toward the shore, too.

I took off so hard and fast, I almost came clear out of the water.

10

Wat are you *two guys* doing?" Daniel asked. Only there was a weird sound to his voice. As if his words carried a disgusted edge, sharper than a knife.

It was right about then that I noticed we were standing a good ten feet up the bank from the water. Everyone's flashlight was on us. And Ted and I were holding on to each other.

I guess it did look kind of strange.

We sprang apart as if we'd been holding on to a hot stove.

"What's going on?" Pepper asked.

"You saw the monster, didn't you?" Zane turned to shine his light on the lake.

Then somebody noticed the fish. Gasps and shouts filled the night. But once everyone had inspected the huge channel cat, their attention returned to us.

"Who screamed?"

"It wasn't a scream," I protested softly. "It was a yell."

"What happened?"

Naturally, Ted—my best friend—pointed straight at me. "It was Kent."

"I didn't scream," I mumbled again. "I yelled."

"There were two screams," Foster pointed out.

Ted made a gulping sound when he swallowed. "Well, Kent screamed and started fighting the water. Then he took off for the bank." He shrugged. "I figured something got him—and whatever it was—well, it was probably coming after me, next."

All the lights turned on me.

"What was it, Kent?"

"What happened?"

I cleared my throat. "Something wet, and cold, and slimy grabbed me . . ." I pointed down. ". . . Right there!"

Everybody sort of cringed and moaned.

"Did it bite you?"

"No. It just . . . it just . . . something kind of hit me." I didn't like all those flashlights on me.

Ted was beside me again. "Something wet, and cold, and slimy touched you?"

"Yeah, it was more like a slap."

Suddenly something slapped my leg. I jumped. I couldn't help it. Then I looked down. Ted held the smaller of our two catfish and whacked me again with the tail.

My shoulders sagged so low, my knuckles could have dragged the ground.

The chuckling seemed to grow. Everybody started pointing and laughing. It's one of those things that . . . well, I guess it really was funny—just as long as it happened to *someone else*.

There was not much to do but join in and laugh with them—after we put our underwear on.

Being the laughingstock wasn't so bad. All the other guys, except for Daniel, let me know that if it had happened to them they would have probably done the same thing. But being the brunt of their teasing—once—was enough. That's why, when Zane saw the lake monster, I never admitted that I saw it, too.

The scream was enough to wake the dead!

We all looked. From far down the bank, a flashlight bobbed and flickered its glow all over the place.

"I saw it!" The shout seemed to come from the light. "I saw it! Come quick! Hurry, before it swims away."

We raced toward Zane's voice. I only "raced" about three paces when I hit a pile of goatheads. Flinching, I stopped dead in my tracks, stood on my left foot, and balanced on the toe of my right.

I hate stickers.

I hopped toward the water a couple of times—just to make sure I was out of the sticker patch—then I raised my foot and pulled the nasty goatheads out.

Only when I took off again, I realized I didn't get all of them. Shining the light to make sure I wouldn't sit down in the stupid things, I found a sandy spot on the bank. I pulled my right foot up in my lap and put the light down beside me so I could see.

By the time I got the stickers out, the others were quite a ways off. Frantic and still yelling, Zane ran from one guy to the next. He shook everybody except Pepper.

"Hurry! Come on. I saw it!"

They followed him a few more feet, then stopped to shine their lights out on the lake.

Tilted to one side and limping, I tried to catch up with them. Then—I decided to just walk.

"It was right there!" Zane's voice cried out. "Just to the left of that bank pole. I saw its eyes."

"Zane, you're always seeing stuff," Daniel's irritated voice growled.

"I swear! They were red or orange. They glowed. I saw it! We were skinny-dipping with . . . with that thing in the lake. We were skinny-dipping with the monster. It was out there . . . with us. Right there!"

Streaks of light danced across the water. Then the moaning and groaning and griping started. All the guys took turns at him with:

"You idiot. You probably saw the light from a boat, across the lake."

"Yeah. You're always seeing stuff, Zane."

"It probably wasn't even a boat. It was just somebody's porch light, reflecting off the water."

"Zane, you're a total knot-head. There's no such thing as a Lake Monster. Between you seeing the Lake Monster and Kent getting attacked by a wild catfish . . . man, this is turning into one *loooong* night."

"I promise!" Zane pleaded. "I saw its eyes. They were red. I'm not lying this time. Honest."

A movement caught the corner of my eye. Halfway to the gang, I stopped dead in my tracks. Without shining the light, I turned toward the lake.

Thirty feet out, and maybe two to three feet below the surface . . .

Two eyes stared at me.

The breath caught in my throat. Every muscle tensed, but I didn't move. I didn't even blink.

The eyes weren't red, though. They had sort of

an orangish glow—almost a dim yellow.

A little shudder raced from my tailbone up to the nape of my neck. It set the little hairs at the base of my skull up on end. I don't know how long I held my breath. I finally had to let it go and suck in a new one. I really *had* seen eyes before!

Zane was right. The thing was out there with us. We were skinny-dipping with the yellow-eyed monster. Then I saw how far apart the eyes were. It didn't matter that we were skinny-dipping. We could have had our bathing suits on . . . we could have had our jeans . . . no, all our clothes . . . it didn't matter. That thing was big enough that it could have swallowed us in one gulp and . . .

You wimp! I told myself. *You're as bad as Zane. There's no such thing as monsters. The light's coming from someplace else.*

I took another breath and stared at the bank, across the lake. No lights danced and shimmered on the ripples. I scanned to the left and then the right. There were no boats. Then I focused back on the spot where I saw the eyes. Sure enough, the light came from beneath the surface. The lake was pretty clear, and I could see the sediment or little particles of dirt and dust scampering before the glow. Then . . . the eyes blinked and flickered.

I didn't mean to slam into Jordan. I hit him so

hard, I almost knocked him flat on the bank. Trouble was, I was sprinting so fast, I just couldn't stop.

"Hey, what's with you?" He stumbled and caught his balance.

"Ah . . . er . . . ah . . . I was just coming to see what all the commotion was." The stammering lie finally made its way out. "What happened? Is Zane okay?"

"Oh, he's having hallucinations again," Jordan answered.

"Yeah," Daniel chimed in. "He saw the Lake Monster."

"We ought to feed *him* to the Lake Monster," Chet scoffed.

"Yeah." Pepper laughed. "Let's do it."

There was a short wrestling match. I mean, really short. After all, Zane was outnumbered six to one. It took only a matter of seconds before Pepper had one arm and Daniel had the other. Foster caught one leg, and despite all Zane's hopping and bouncing around, Chet finally captured his free foot. Jordan cheered them on as they stretched Zane out between them and made their way out, until they were about ankle deep in the water. Then they started swinging him back and forth.

"One!"

There was something inside of me that wanted

to yell: *"Stop. Don't throw him in. I saw the monster's eyes."*

"Two!"

But there was something else inside of me that said: *"Keep your mouth shut, Kent. They're not going to believe you. You'll end up in the lake, too."* So . . . with one part of my insides fighting the other part . . . I just stood there.

"Three!"

Even spinning and flailing and jerking and flopping, it was downright amazing how far Zane flew. Clothes and all, he hit the water with a splash that was better than any cannonball we could do in the pool. Still, somehow—the instant he hit the water, he managed to get his bearings. In the blink of an eye he was on his feet and charging toward the bank. Well, maybe not toward the bank, but at least *away from* the lake and the monster. He shot past us so fast that we hadn't even picked up our flashlights by the time he was halfway to the campfire.

As the rest of the guys headed back up the hill, I slipped off toward where I saw the eyes. There had to be some explanation. There wasn't really a monster living in Cedar Lake. But I knew I saw something. If I could just see it again . . . If I could just figure out what . . .

"Where are you headed, Kent?" Ted called.

I stopped. His flashlight made me blink. I shined my light at his eyes.

"Ah . . . I . . . I lost something," I stammered. "Yeah, I lost something on the bank."

"What was it? I'll help you find it."

Frantic to cover up my lie, I dug into my pocket. Sure enough, there was a quarter in there.

"It was my lucky quarter," I lied.

"Lucky quarter?"

"Yes. I . . . ah . . . always carry it when I go fishing."

"Want me to come and help you look?"

"Nah. It's no big deal."

The light bounced in Ted's hand when he shrugged. I was glad he turned and headed toward the camp with the rest of the guys. Lying is *not* cool. It always made me feel kind of creepy or ashamed inside. But this was different. I just couldn't tell.

Ted was my best friend, and I really wanted to confide in him. But . . .

Maybe I could tell Mom and Dad when I got home.

Maybe not.

Maybe I just couldn't tell a single soul—not until I knew for sure what I had really seen.

11

I didn't see the eyes again.

I finally gave up and went back to camp, but I didn't get any sleep. About an hour or so after the sun came up, we had hot dogs and marshmallows for breakfast.

Zane didn't eat anything. Partly because he was still pouting about everybody making fun of him. And partly because he was still all wet and soggy. It's hard to be sociable when you're dripping and sloshing around in wet clothes. Ted asked me if I found my lucky quarter. I showed him the one I discovered in my pocket, and that was the end of it. But I still felt guilty about lying to him. I felt even worse about not taking up for Zane.

When we finished eating, everyone drank a pop. Then we started packing stuff up so it would be ready for the dads to load while we rode the horses back home. We were so tired, all thought of riding around the lake was forgotten.

When everything was in a neat pile, we each drank another pop so we could put the fire out.

Guys know how to put out a campfire.

It's one of those things that nobody—not even your dad or the older guys—have to tell you. You just know.

We formed a circle.

The embers and coals hissed and crackled. Steam and smoke swirled into the morning air. Daniel and Chet got in a sword fight with their streams, so the rest of us moved away and stood shoulder to shoulder on the other side. Just to make sure it was completely out, Ted poured the water from the minnow buckets and ice chests on it, too. Then we got our horses and rode to Ted's house to clean the fish. Mr. Aikman came out to help us. When he saw the big one, his eyes lit up. He went back inside and got his fish scales. The thing weighed out at thirteen pounds, eight ounces. He weighed a couple of the others. One went five even. Another went seven pounds and fifteen ounces.

Before we started cleaning the fish, Mr. Aikman made us go in and wash our hands at the kitchen sink. (Guess he knew how to put out a campfire, too.)

We put a *big* mess of fish in Ted's refrigerator.

Mr. Aikman took Ted and me to help him load the camping stuff in the back of the pickup. Once it was all delivered, I rode Duke home. Mom left a note on the front door, telling me she was off showing a house to a client. I latched the door, took a quick shower, and crawled into bed.

I didn't even have the pillow fluffed around my head when the phone rang. It was Pepper. He told me that we were having the fish fry tonight and asked if it was okay with my parents. I told him they were both gone, but I knew Dad didn't have to work tonight, so I thought we should be able to be there.

As soon as I hit the sheets, the phone rang again. This time it was Jordan.

"Let's go out and dig the trench for the telegraph line." His voice was all bright and cheerful.

"Huh?" I hadn't made it to bed yet. Still, I was so tired from working all day cutting bank poles, and staying up all night fishing . . . well, I guess I was already half asleep.

"The trench for the telegraph line," he repeated. "We need to bury the thing. Our dads have hit it so many times with the lawnmowers, and we've spliced it with electrical tape so often that it will short out if we leave it exposed to the elements. We have to bury it. We have an adequate supply of PVC pipe left over from when we built the house. It's out behind the horse barn. We'll put the line in it so it won't be exposed to the weather, then bury the entire thing and—"

"Jordan."

"What?"

"Didn't you stay up fishing all night with the rest of us?"

"Yes."

"Aren't you sleepy?"

"No, not in the least."

"Well, I am! Let's do it some other time. Besides that, I don't even know Morse code. What am I gonna do with a telegraph line?"

"It's quite simple. I've a book that I can loan you. Once we have the line buried—"

"Not today, Jordan," I cut him off. "Some other time."

"Well, fine!" he huffed. "I'll just do it myself."

"Good! You do that, Jordan."

I went back to bed. Trouble was, even after being up all night—now—I was wide awake. I tossed and turned and flipped and flopped.

Every time I closed my eyes, I could see those yellow eyes staring at me. I just couldn't get it out of my mind. Finally I sat up on the edge of the bed and started talking to myself.

"All right. You know you're going back out to look for the Lake Monster, right?"

"Right."

"But you can't let anybody know, right?"

"Right."

"So how do you expect to get out of the house without Mom and Dad hearing the alarm? Even if it doesn't screech and wake the whole country, it still makes that beeping sound when you punch the buttons. How can I get out of the house without . . ."

Elbows on my legs, I slumped over and rested my chin in my hands. Finally, unable to sleep and with nothing else to do, I got up and staggered into the living room. I flipped the TV on, but there was nothing but talk shows and soap operas. So I started looking through Dad's videotapes.

Suddenly I blinked. Then I blinked again.

Beverly Hills Cop II was on the top of the video tape pile I was looking at. It almost seemed to stare back at me. An old Eddie Murphy film, it was one of Dad's favorite tapes. I don't know how many times I had watched it with him. A sly smile tugged at my face when I remembered the part when Eddie Murphy used the gum wrapper to fool the alarm system.

I raced to the kitchen cabinet where we kept the gum. I unwrapped two pieces, popped them in my mouth, then smoothed the foil out on the bar.

Smacking my gum, I raced to the front door and looked out to make sure Mom wasn't through showing the house and had come home.

All I saw was Jordan. He had a shovel and was working on the trench for his telegraph wire. I scampered back to the cabinet and got the gum wrappers. On my way down the hall, I punched in the code to set the alarm.

"So what did you do today?" Mom asked when she came home. She looked a little surprised to see me awake, I think.

"Oh, nothing much." I shrugged. "Just watched TV a while."

"I thought you'd be asleep."

I shrugged again. "Wasn't sleepy."

She looked a little suspicious when I said that. Then she put her purse on the coffee table. "Oh, by the way, Mrs. Hamilton got hold of me on the cell phone. You did know about the fish fry at Pepper's house tonight."

"Yes. Did you tell Dad?"

"Called him at work. Said it would be fine and he should be home around six."

The fish fry was fun. Our parents visited and seemed to have a good time. Our dads were proud of all the fish we had caught. Just as always at the Hamiltons' house, the food was delicious. When we finished eating, we all went swimming.

The Hamiltons had a big pool. We played tag for a while. It was a blast having our parents play with us. But with so many people in the water, it was nothing at all to find somebody to tag. Then we played Marco Polo. One by one, our parents kind of drifted off to sit in the lawn chairs and talk.

We swam and played tag and took turns dunking one another. When we headed home, I knew I was going to sleep like a log that night.

When we got home, I brushed my teeth and went straight to bed. I pulled the sheet over me and reached over to pat the nightstand. The two pieces of gum, wrapped in foil, were there and waiting. All I had to do was stay up until Mom and Dad were asleep.

I glanced at the clock beside my bed. Eleven fifteen. Late as it was, it shouldn't take long at all.

12

When I yawned and stretched and finally forced my eyes open, I glanced at the clock beside my bed.

Twelve fifteen.

It was eleven fifteen when I went to sleep. I'd only been out for an hour and . . .

Something wasn't right. I sat up and yawned again. There was light coming into my room. I tugged at the shade, then let go. It spun and whizzed open. My eyes snapped shut as tight as I could get them.

It wasn't twelve fifteen at night. It was noon. I'd slept for . . . for . . .

I was still too sleepy to even count. I staggered into the kitchen.

"Morning, sleepyhead," Mom greeted from her office as I waddled past. I backed up so I could see her through the doorway. "Hope you're caught up on your sleep. Fixed you a sandwich. It's in the fridge. There are some chips in the pantry."

I missed out on going to the lake last night

because I fell asleep. I guess the rest of the guys slept in, too. The phone never rang. I ate, then watched TV for a while. At four I went back to my room for a nap. I had to be able to stay awake tonight.

At supper Dad reminded me that our scuba classes started week after next. He suggested that I get my regulator and tank out of the closet, clean them, and make sure everything was in good working order. Since most of the guys were going to be gone on vacation, I was looking forward to having something to do. I promised him that I would. Then Dad helped me with the dishes and we went to watch TV. I was wide awake, but I kept yawning. Maybe it was contagious and Mom and Dad would get sleepy, just watching me.

I thought they would never go to bed.

Really-n-truly, I never expected to see the Lake Monster. First off, I didn't believe in monsters. Then, too, I'd had enough time to convince myself that whatever Zane and I thought we had seen . . . well, whatever it was, we really *hadn't* seen it.

Sneaking out of the house was something I had never ever done before—so I just had to do it.

The instant I shut the door to my bedroom, I shot straight to the window. A little white wire came through the ceiling and down to a tiny plastic rectangle on the edge of the window frame. There was a magnet inside. Another little plastic rectangle was attached, with screws, to the part of the window that went up and down. I stood there, holding my breath, until I heard the little *beep, beep, beep* that came from the alarm box in the hall. That meant Dad had set the thing for the night.

Careful as could be, I eased the flattened gum wrapper between the two magnets. Holding it in place with my right hand, I raised the window with my left. The foil stuck to the magnet on the window frame. I guess it fooled the alarm into thinking that it was still closed.

Once that was done, I turned out my light and waited. Mom and Dad had a TV in their bedroom. It stayed on for about twenty minutes, then everything got quiet. I gave it another twenty minutes before I sneaked down the hall.

Holding my breath, and quiet as could be, I leaned an ear toward their bedroom door. There wasn't a sound. After waiting a little longer, I listened again, then tiptoed back to my room. Using both hands and moving so slowly that the window screen wouldn't scrape or squeak, I lifted it out of the frame and placed it gently on the floor. Only then did I take a deep breath. Careful and slow, so as not to disturb the gum wrapper, I eased through the opening and crept to the edge of our yard.

I'm not scared of the dark.

At least, that's what I kept telling myself. There was no moon—not even a little sliver. The gentle breeze had just enough push to rustle the dry blades of Johnsongrass. The sounds made me pause and turn my light toward them. Moving carefully and shining the beam at each spot before I took a step, I finally made my way to the place where I saw the eyes. Sure there were no snakes crawling around the bank, I flipped the flashlight off.

Water sloshed and patted against the shore. From across the lake, I heard a car horn and the sound of an outboard motor near the marina. The boat must have come from this side of the lake, because the waves started rolling louder and closer near my feet. It takes a while for a wake to make its way into shore. Still, I couldn't help but flip the light on again, to make sure it was just water sloshing.

A little rock knoll stuck up about twenty feet to my left. It was back a ways from the water and would give me a higher spot where I could see better. It would also get me farther from the water snakes or whatever else might be lurking around the shore. I climbed to the top of it and found a flat rock to sit on. Once again I turned my flashlight off—determined, this time, not to risk scaring away the Lake Monster.

The thought made me bite down on my bottom lip and snort.

"Lake Monster," I scoffed, whispering inside my own head. "How stupid can you get? There's no monster."

"But whatever it was," I argued with myself, "it might see the light and you'll *never* know."

There were crickets chirping and little crunchy sounds that came from the dry grass at times. Convinced the "crunchies" were mice, I kept the light off. Something rustled some cattails out in the water. For only an instant I flipped my light on and decided it was just the waves.

Last year, for my birthday, Dad had given me a nice dive watch. It had hands that glowed in the dark. It was only ten forty-five. I'd give it until midnight.

The next time I looked, it was ten forty-nine. Maybe I'd give it until eleven thirty.

The rock where I'd picked to sit was smooth and flat. At first it was comfortable. After about thirty minutes I decided it was the hardest rock I ever met. I kept shifting my weight—leaning from one side to the other—but nothing seemed to help. My bottom ached and no matter what I tried, there wasn't any way to get comfortable.

At eleven forty I just couldn't take it anymore. I struggled to my feet and set the flashlight down so I could rub my aching bottom and my legs. As I raised up and leaned back so I could massage the sore spot in the small of my back, I looked out on the lake.

Eyes looked back at me!

About three feet beneath the surface, they were bright and burning. Not orange or yellow this time, they glowed almost white-hot as it stared at me.

Slow and steady, they moved beneath the surface. They were coming this way!

13

Chances were, I'd probably break my neck if I tried to jump from this pile of rock and go running for home. I'd more than likely end up lying on the ground, with two broken legs. Totally helpless—all I'd be able to do was wait for the monster to crawl out of the water and come after me.

There were all sorts of stories about the Monster of Cedar Lake. Late at night, fishermen had seen its eyes. They had tales about it chewing through trotlines as smooth as a hot knife cuts butter. One fisherman had told that something grabbed his boat anchor and dragged him and his boat halfway across the lake before the rope broke. People had seen the eyes—glowing beneath the surface of the water. But nobody had ever seen the monster. And even seeing the eyes . . . well, the stories were few and far between. It just didn't happen that often. I couldn't believe that I saw them again tonight.

Trouble with seeing them was . . . if this thing kept coming, straight at me . . . well, I was going to see the Monster of Cedar Lake—"up close and personal." That was something I simply *did not* want to do.

The way I figured it, there wasn't much choice. I was going to have to jump from the pile of rocks and try to make it to the house. Maybe—even if I broke my leg, I could still drag myself and . . .

What if this pile of rock I'd picked to watch from was its lair—its nest? Maybe there was a cave under the rock. Maybe . . .

Legs tensed, knees bent, I was just ready to jump when the eyes slowly turned to my left.

Motionless, I held my breath until I finally realized the eyes were moving away. They were headed toward the end of the lake. Trying to climb down off the pile of rock, and still keep from losing sight of the eyes, was a challenge.

Once on flat ground I had to run to catch up with the monster. Jogging in the dark was kind of tricky, but I stayed between the lake and the grass line. Even at that, I hit the water a couple of times, but I didn't slow down.

I followed the eyes for nearly a quarter of a mile. When they stopped and turned back to look at the bank, I froze in my tracks. I was on Mrs. Baum's place, not far from the little work shed that stood in the middle of her yard. With my luck, she'd

probably come out of her house and start screaming at me to get off her land.

There were two huge cottonwood trees in front
of me. Hard telling how old the things were,
because they were enormous. About twenty yards
apart, their limbs stretched out over the lake and
toward each other, until the branches touched. The
trunk on the nearest tree was gigantic. It would be
the perfect place to hide and watch.

I only took a step or two toward it when the eyes
blinked. They were coming straight for the trees.

Instantly I dropped to one knee. I'd hide right
here in the open. This was close enough.

The eyes moved nearer. Closer. Whatever it was,
the thing was going to come out on the bank, right
between the two huge cottonwood trees.

But the eyes stayed under the water.

As I watched, my shoulders sagged and my head
tilted so far to one side, I almost lost my balance.
It didn't come out. I couldn't see it. I couldn't hear
a splash.

Ted and I had run bank pole lines just up the
shore from here. It was shallow. The shore sloped
gently, and there were no canyons or streams hid-
den beneath the surface. It had to come up.

Between the two trees, and right before it
touched the bank . . . the eyes disappeared.

I waited and waited. Finally I eased to my feet —just in case I had to run—and shone my flashlight at the spot between the two big cottonwoods. If it was there, it would see me for sure. I'd have to get away quick.

There was nothing. Just the two trees, the bank, and the water. No eyes. No huge, lurking, lumbering shape. Nothing.

Frowning, I moved closer.

Maybe it closed its eyes, turned around, and swam back out into the lake.

The closer I got to the water, the tighter my legs felt. They trembled and hesitated longer and longer between each step. My feet touched the ground like they were searching for something— like a twig or an eggshell might suddenly snap or crack beneath my sneakers. When I realized what I was doing, I felt like such a wimp.

Inch at a time, I finally found myself standing between the two giant cottonwood trees. There were no tracks. Not even a wet spot where something had stepped or dragged itself out onto the shore.

The strange hissing noise behind me sent a chill shooting up my spine. I was a good twenty yards up the bank before I even realized my feet were running.

Stopping, I made myself turn back and shine my light. Again . . . there was nothing there. Just the little, rickety work shed in front of Mrs. Baum's house.

Another hiss came. This time the panic didn't grab me. I turned my head, listening. When the sound came a third time, I aimed my flashlight at the work shed. I took a step toward it.

The trembling across my shoulders and up my back almost shook the flashlight from my hand. More than anything, I wanted to run home. Fingers so tight around the handle that my knuckles hurt, I turned the light off. But I *did* keep my thumb poised above the off/on switch and kept it aimed toward the sound.

Then . . .

The door creaked. It opened.

Eyes wide, I held my breath.

"Who's there?" A loud shrill voice knifed through the night. "Who's out there?"

It was Mrs. Baum. I wanted to turn the light on and make sure, but if I turned the light on, she'd see me. Alone in the dark, I dropped to one knee and hunkered low to the ground. The door creaked again.

I couldn't see a thing without my light. And there was no way I was going to switch it back on.

"I've got my shotgun," the high, shrill voice threatened. "If I see anybody out there, I'll fill your hind end with buckshot."

Yep. There was no mistaking that voice. It was Mrs. Baum's. I'd heard that shrill high screech, more than once, telling me to get my horse out from in front of her house.

The door slammed. Inside the little shed, I could hear clunking, thumping sounds. Someone was moving things as if looking for something.

I'd done some dumb stuff. I guess all of us do. The first thing that came to mind was trying to jump Bobcat Canyon on my bicycle. But there had been others, far too many to flutter through my mind's eye at this particular second.

The vision that did come was terrifying.

In the dark . . . inside my head . . . I could almost see grouchy old Mrs. Baum . . . armed with a shotgun.

Like I said, I'd done some dumb stuff. That didn't mean I was a *total idiot*.

I took off!

Forget going down to the lake where the ground was smooth. Forget shining the light before each step to make sure there wasn't a snake.

Go home!

I couldn't have run faster if the Lake Monster

itself had been breathing down the back of my neck.

Things were going great . . . until . . .

I forgot about the fence at the edge of the Ferguson place. From then on, it was downhill all the way. A total disaster.

14

G rounded?"

"I already said that, Ted. Grounded."

"Grounded?"

I held the phone away from my ear and glared at it like it was the most stupid thing in the world. Since Ted had called less than a minute ago to see if I could ride over to Bobcat Canyon and have a war with the guys, it was the third time that "Grounded?" had shrieked through the phone and into my ear. It was the fourth time I'd had to repeat the word.

"Ted. You got something stuck in your ear? Grounded. That's spelled G-R-O-U-N-D-E-D. Got it? I can't leave the house. I can't have company over. I'm not even supposed to talk on the phone. Mom said I could tell you and you could tell the other guys so they wouldn't be calling or coming over." I sucked in a deep breath because I was about out of air after getting all that in.

"What did you do?"

"Well . . ." I paused long enough to glance over

my shoulder. Mom stood in the doorway with her arms folded. "Well . . . I never sneaked out of the house before. I just wanted to see if I could do it. You know."

"And you got caught?"

"Yes."

"So how long are you grounded?"

"Well, Mom and Dad don't think that was the 'real' reason I sneaked out of the house. So . . . well, if I don't tell them . . . well, like forever . . . sort of."

"Why *did* you sneak out?"

I glanced back again. Mom had her arms folded. Her eyebrows were arched so high they almost looked like part of her hairline.

"Mom wants me to get off the phone, Ted."

"I didn't hear anything."

"Ah . . . right."

There was a long pause on the other end of the line. "She's in the room, listening—right?"

"That's it. Be sure and tell the other guys not to call or come by."

"Okay, Kent. See you later. I *got* to know what's going on."

Mom stood there, staring at me for a long time after I hung up the phone. Finally she sighed, gave a little shrug, and went back to her office.

Around ten thirty the telephone rang. From the other room I could hear her talking. There was a long silence, then she came to my room.

"I have to meet Mr. and Mrs. Blevins and show them some houses," she said. "You can watch TV while I'm gone, but do *not* leave the house or answer the phone."

I nodded, letting her know I understood. But inside my head, I was thinking that if one of the guys called . . . how would she know?

It's really spooky when mothers can read your mind.

"By the way," she said, stopping in the doorway and not even looking back at me, "I'm expecting a couple of phone calls. When I get home, they should be on the answering machine. If they're not, I'll know someone's been on the telephone. Since your father is at work—guess who that leaves?"

Like I said—spooky.

When she drove off, I found a book to read. I hadn't even gotten through Chapter One when I heard the pounding at the front door. Figuring she had forgotten something, I hopped up to go let her in.

"All right. What were you doing and how did you get caught?" Ted and Jordan brushed past me and into the living room.

"I'm grounded!" I yelped, glancing outside to see if Mom's car had gone. The driveway and road were empty. I slammed the door behind them. "You two can't come in. She will—"

"Your mom just drove off," Ted said. "Soon as I heard you were grounded, I came over."

"He's been helping me with the trench for the telegraph line." Jordan beamed.

"But . . . but . . ."

"Don't stand there stammering," Ted grumped. He stuck his thumb at the side of the curtain and opened it just enough so he could peek out. "How did you get grounded? What did you do? And talk quick, before your mom comes back."

"Remember the other night when Zane told everybody about seeing the monster?" I began. "You all made fun of him and threw him in the lake, remember?"

"Yeah," they both answered.

"Well." I hesitated. Silence swept through the room so thick I could almost feel it. "Well," I went on, "I saw it, too!"

I don't know how long it took, but I told them the whole story. Every single detail, from seeing the eyes, to rigging the alarm, to hearing the sounds from the work shed in front of Mrs. Baum's house and having her scream at me.

To my surprise, Jordan was evidently still listening. "So how did you get caught?" he asked.

I held my arms out, then lifted my shirt to show them all the scratches. "I forgot about the Fergusons' barbed-wire fence. I was running so fast, I almost ripped myself to pieces trying to get loose. Then I jumped through the window and pulled it down behind me—only . . . well . . ."

"You forgot about the gum wrapper," Ted finished what I was trying to say.

All I could do was feel kind of sick and stupid inside when I nodded my head.

"Little wonder they doubt the integrity of your story." Jordan heaved a sigh. "All the evidence—the torn clothing, the scratches—everything points to something far more involved and insidious than simply tampering with the alarm."

Ted and I looked at him. Then we looked at each other. Ted finally blinked a couple of times, really hard, then rolled his eyes.

"I got no idea what Jordan just said, but I think he's right. You come in all ripped up and muddy—there's no way they're going to buy a story about you stepping outside, just to see if you could. So . . . the thing we need to do now is figure how to get you out of it."

"It won't work."

"What do you mean, it won't work? I haven't even come up with an idea yet."

"Whatever it is, it won't work. Mom *knows* if I lie to her."

"You can't lie to her, but I can." Ted grinned. "Jordan and I will come up with something. When we get back, just play along—no matter what—okay?"

"Okay."

Mom and Dad got home about six. Mom started supper. Dad had me go with him to the garage. He double-checked my scuba tank and regulator— just to make sure I had it cleaned and ready like he had told me to. Then he let the air out of both tanks, started the compressor, and refilled them.

"Be a shame if you can't go to the scuba classes with me next Friday . . . because you're grounded."

I didn't say anything.

"Yep, real shame. I think Charles Korbin is bringing his daughter. She's that cute little blonde. About your age? You remember her, don't you?"

I still didn't say anything.

There was something about the way Dad was carrying on that told me all he was trying to do was get me talking. Trying to get me loosened up—so I'd slip and tell him why I was outside last night.

"Oh, I'm sure you remember Krissi. Last summer?

At the fire-department picnic? You spent about two hours playing tag and chasing her all over the park. Charles told me she's really grown over the past year. You know . . . matured? Filled out? Fact is, she bought a new bathing suit for the scuba class. Old Charlie is a bit concerned about letting her wear it. It's a little pink two-piece bathing suit. He thinks it's too skimpy for her to be wearing in public. What do you think, Kent?"

Dad almost suckered me in with that one. I was just about to blurt out something like:

"I *definitely* think she should wear it."

If it hadn't been for Ted, I probably would have. Right about then, he stuck his head in the door.

"Mr. Morgan?" he called. "May I speak with you a moment, sir?" Then, like he didn't even expect me to be around, he gave a quick nod in my direction. "Oh, hi, Kent."

Ted stood there, holding something behind him. He moved into the garage, smiling from ear to ear.

"I found it, Kent. It's okay. You can tell them now."

My mouth flopped open, but not a single sound came out. Ted told me to play along with his story.

Playing along didn't mean making it up! At this rate I'd be grounded for the rest of my life.

15

Ted produced a rod and reel from behind his back. He told Dad that his father gave it to him for Christmas. "I made Kent promise not to tell anybody that I lost it," Ted said. "I was afraid my dad would kill me if he found out. Your son gave me his word. I guess he kept it, because he's still grounded."

Dad frowned and tilted his head to one side.

"Kent promised he'd help me find it and not tell anybody."

The way Dad's forehead wrinkled, I could tell he was thinking on it—only he didn't quite buy it.

"That's why you didn't tell me?"

When Dad looked at me, all I could do was duck my head.

"I probably would have told," Ted stepped between us. "Your son sure is a man of his word, Mr. Morgan. But now that I've found my rod and reel . . . well, it wasn't his fault. Please don't be mad at him for something *I* did."

It seemed like an eternity that Dad stood there

staring at us. Finally he sighed. "I'll talk to your mom."

Ted and I held our breath. The second the screen bounced shut, I wheeled on him.

"How did you come up with that one? And how can you lie with such a straight face?"

"It wasn't a total lie." Ted smiled. "I told him it was a Christmas present from Dad. It was. I told him I lost it. I did."

"Huh?"

"Jordan took it, hid it, then we went and found it. So . . . it wasn't a total lie."

All I could do was shake my head.

"Once we're sure you're not grounded anymore, Jordan and I will call the guys and get everything set for another fishing trip tomorrow night. We'll stretch the bank poles out so the last one is down where you saw the eyes disappear and . . ."

The screen door opened. Both of us stood there, looking as innocent as could be.

Being grounded, especially in the summer, was horrible.

Being ungrounded . . . that was great.

Even though I was getting ready to spend the whole night fishing and watching for the Monster of Cedar Lake, I still got up at six the next morning. Before Mom left to go show some houses, she called Dad at the fire station and reminded him of Samantha Hamilton's wedding shower the following night. About ten she headed off. Before she left, I reminded her of the fishing trip, and that it was my turn to bring the pop. She promised she'd get some at the store.

I fed Duke and made sure he had fresh water. Then I cleaned out my tackle box and had all my fishing stuff ready and sitting on the front porch before noon. I even wrapped my bathing trunks in a towel to take along. No more of that skinny-dipping stuff for me.

When Mom got home from work she brought us each a hamburger and some fries. She'd also stopped at the store and picked up five six-packs of pop. We ate, then got two coolers from the garage, iced down the pop, and set the chests on the front porch with my fishing gear.

Mom said she had to go back and show her clients two more houses. She seemed sort of happy and excited, because she was pretty sure they were going to buy one.

With Duke fed and all my stuff ready, there wasn't much else to do but sit around and wait. I hated waiting. I flipped on the TV, but didn't even bother to watch it. The noise made it feel like the house wasn't so empty. I curled up on the couch and went right to sleep.

I felt like I'd just closed my eyes when the phone rang. But when I glanced at the clock over the TV, I figured I'd been out for two hours. The phone rang again.

"Hello?"

"Kent. Ted. Guess the fishing trip's off."

"What?" I yelped. I yanked the phone away and glared at it, as if I couldn't believe what it just said. When I stuck it back to my ear, Ted was already talking.

". . . and man, don't scream on the phone like that. You almost blew my eardrum out."

"Why's the fishing trip off?"

"Haven't you been listening to the TV?" Ted asked.

"No."

"There's, like, storms coming through. Big ones. We'll have to go tomorrow night. Mom's talking about going to the cellar. Gotta go. Bye."

Sure enough, Ted was right. Every channel had tornado warnings on the screen. Meteorologists interrupted soap operas to show Doppler radar and warnings flashed over the top of the picture. The line of storms was still a few counties away, but they were headed in this direction.

I sure wished Mom or Dad would come home.

It was only about ten minutes later when the phone rang again. I snatched it up and stuck it to my ear.

"Hello?"

"Kent, your dad just called on my cell phone. He wants us to come to the fire station until these storms blow over. Close the windows. Lock the doors. I'll meet you in front of the house. Scoot!"

"Yes, ma'am."

I scooted. The windows were already closed. I ran outside and opened the gate to Duke's pen. That way, if the storm did get too close, he wouldn't be trapped in that little tiny stall. I locked the back door, raced through the house, turned off the TV, and locked the front door just as Mom drove up. She flung the car door open and I hopped in.

Only we didn't head to town. We turned right.

"Where are we going?"

"We have to pick up Emma. With these storms coming, I don't want her in that old house all alone."

My luck was really on a downhill slide. First off, no fishing trip. Then—Mrs. Baum. With my luck, she had recognized me the other night and would tell Mom.

Mrs. Baum was waiting in her driveway. She had a paper sack in her hand. I hopped in the back—hoping and praying that she hadn't recognized me.

If she did, she never said a word.

The community storm shelter was in the basement of the fire department. Dad waited for us outside the back door, where the parking lot was. He gave Mrs. Baum a big hug, kissed Mom on the cheek, and ruffled my hair.

"This thing will probably blow over, like most of 'em do. It *is* a big storm system, though. Lots of straight wind and some hail. I just feel safer with you here. Come on."

Quite a few people were already downstairs. There were about eight old couples. A number of the firefighters' families were there and some other people with kids. Only about twenty chairs lined the walls. Mom found an empty one for Mrs. Baum, then sat on the floor next to her, talking about grown-up stuff, like bills and the cost of living and all that junk.

Impatient and bored, I shifted nervously from one foot to the other. I was just getting ready to ask if I could go upstairs to see what Dad was doing, when someone tapped me on the shoulder.

"Kent? Kent Morgan? Is that you? I haven't seen you since the picnic last year."

It was Krissi Korbin.

I blinked. Then blinked again. What her dad had told my dad . . . well, it wasn't quite true. She hadn't changed a little. She'd changed a *lot*.

She *was* cute.

Mom introduced her to Mrs. Baum, and Krissi sat on the floor next to them. For some strange reason, Krissi and Mrs. Baum seemed to hit it off from the very first. The three of them talked and visited and laughed. After a while, I got to feeling really left out.

I guess Mrs. Baum finally noticed. She glanced up and smiled at me.

"Oh, Kent. I almost forgot. Remember I told you the other night that I'd fix some chocolate chip cookies?" She reached to the floor beside her and picked up the paper sack. "Here you go. I think there's enough to share with your mom and this beautiful young lady, too."

I thought Pepper Hamilton's mother made the best chocolate chip cookies in the country.

Wrong.

When it came to cookies, Emma Baum had the Hamiltons beat all to pieces.

We all visited and munched on the wonderful

cookies. Mom excused herself when she spotted the people who had just bought the house from her. Then Krissi and Mrs. Baum got to visiting. Then they started whispering to each other. Every now and then they would glance at me, giggle, and whisper some more.

It made me feel really self-conscious and uncomfortable. So I went upstairs to see what Dad and the other firefighters were doing.

It was around ten thirty when the storms passed. Most of the bad ones went to the north of us. Dad's shift wasn't over until eleven, so Mom and I got Mrs. Baum and headed home. There were lots of small limbs and stuff on the roads, but other than that I couldn't see much damage.

As we drove, I really wanted to ask Mrs. Baum what she and Krissi had been talking about when they kept looking at me and giggling. I just didn't have the nerve. But when we got to her house . . .

"Kent," Mom said, turning the engine off. "Walk Emma to the door and make sure everything's okay in the house." She reached over and opened the glove compartment. "I'll take a quick walk around the outside and see if there's any storm damage."

Together, Mrs. Baum and I peeked in each of the rooms. In the kitchen she made me take six more chocolate chip cookies, then she walked with me back to the front door.

"What were you and Krissi giggling about?" I blurted out.

Mrs. Baum smiled. I couldn't help notice the little twinkle in her eye. "You."

I felt the heat rush to my cheeks. I was just going to ask her what they were saying about me when Mom stepped onto the porch.

"Things are fine out here, Emma. You need anything else before we head home?"

"Nope. Doing fine, Elizabeth. Thanks for picking me up. Kent, I'll talk to you again sometime," she added with a wink.

I wanted to know—*now*. But I guess she could tell I didn't want to talk about it in front of Mom.

As soon as we got home, I went to check on Duke. He galloped up from the pasture and shoved his nose in the food bucket that I brought him. I took a quick look at the barn and pen. Sure that everything was all right, I headed back to the house.

I waited for Dad in the garage. While I was standing there, I glanced down at my scuba tank. I felt the smile tug at my ears.

Pink two-piece bathing suit.

I could hardly wait for underwater rescue classes to start next week.

16

Last night I went to sleep with peaceful visions of Krissi Korbin swimming around in her pink two-piece bathing suit.

I guess that's why the next morning came as such a shock.

I wiggled and squirmed a while, then finally sat up on the edge of my bed. As soon as I got my eyes opened and stopped yawning long enough to see, I glanced out the window. There were limbs and trash all over the side yard. I threw on some clothes and trotted outside to see if Duke was okay. I spotted him munching grass in the pasture and swishing at flies with his tail. My horse was fine, but two sheets of tin had been ripped from the roof of his shed. Next to the corral, a big tree limb had snapped and landed on the fence. I could see where the wood was all white and shiny. Frowning, I remembered feeding him the night before and not seeing anything wrong.

Were you so busy thinking about Krissi that you

didn't even notice the barn was messed up? You did-
n't see the broken fence?

Before I could even answer myself, I shook my
head. There was no way I could have missed that.

When I walked around the other side of the
house, I saw a couple of trees that had fallen over,
up by the road.

Mom and Dad were drinking their coffee when
I flew through the back door. I guess my eyes were
wide and my mouth was gaping open, because
Dad answered before I even had a chance to ask.

"Another line of storm rolled through, just
before daylight."

"A second storm? I didn't hear a thing," I confessed.

"Wasn't much thunder or lightning—just
wind."

"Lots of wind," Mom added.

Dad took a sip of his coffee. "Planned to spend
my day off fishing. From the looks of things, probably take most of the day to get it cleaned up
around here." He shrugged and took another sip
from his cup. "Well, maybe I can get a little fishing
in with you boys tonight. You wouldn't mind if I
spent a few minutes at your campout, would you?"

I shook my head. "I'm sure it would be fine with

the guys. Might even see if Mr. Aikman wants to come, too."

"Be good for you to spend some time with your son," Mom said. "You might even—" Suddenly she broke off. She blinked a couple of times, then her eyes got kind of big. "Oh, my gosh. The dinner and wedding shower for Samantha Hamilton is supposed to be tonight. They were going to have it outside in their garden."

Dad blinked back at her. "That's right! Carl and Pepper have been working on a gazebo. You better go and call. See if they had as much damage over on the Point as we did. If they need our help, we can always clean up around here tomorrow."

While Mom was on the phone, Dad and I went to check the shingles on the roof. It wasn't long before she came out to join us.

"They had wind damage. Their gazebo is all right, but the yard's a total mess."

"Is there anything we can do to help?" Dad asked. Mom shook her head and explained that Pepper's folks decided, even with the whole neighborhood pitching in, they couldn't get it cleaned up and ready by tonight. So she called their preacher to see if they could use the church banquet room. Mom was supposed to check back around noon to see if they needed any help.

We spent the rest of the day picking up limbs that were scattered all over the yard and pasture. Dad went to town and got some tin to fix Duke's barn and three boards for the corral fence.

When he got back he found his chain saw in the garage, and I helped him cut the trees off the fence up by the road and get the big limb off Duke's corral. Even cut into small logs, the green wood was heavy and hard to lift. We put the big stuff in the back of his truck, then drove down to add that to the pile Mom and I had made in one of the small ravines. We didn't eat lunch until four that afternoon. After that we rested a few minutes and went to put the new tin on Duke's roof.

I was almost near worn out by the time Ted and Mr. Aikman showed up. While our dads talked, Ted and I went after my fishing stuff.

"No shad gizzards or cut bait," Ted told me as we walked back to where our dads were. "The bait shop was out. Didn't have time to go shoot some with my bow and arrow, because we spent the whole day picking up tree limbs and replacing some tin on the hay barn. Dad got two extra cartons of worms. Figured you, Jordan, and I could go a little early and catch some perch for cut bait."

"Does Pepper get to come?" I asked.

"Think so." Ted nodded. "The shower's just a grown-up party. Yesterday he told me that he'd go fishing with us. But . . . that was before the storm and the mess it made out of their yard."

It was almost dark by the time everyone got there and we had our camp set up. Chet and Daniel brought a tarp to put under the tents and sleeping bags. The ground was still pretty damp from the rain the night before. While they did that, the rest of us found some semidry wood for the fire. Pepper was the last to get there.

He pulled his horse to a stop, right between the tents. Shaking his head, he leaned forward and rested his forearm on the saddle horn.

"You have no idea how happy I am to be here." He sighed. "It's like totally crazy around my house. Everybody's running in circles and goin' nuts. I'm just glad to get out of there. I wish Samantha had eloped instead of going through all this shower stuff."

He twisted around in the saddle, reaching for something behind him. I kind of leaned to the side so I could see what he was after. There were two bags of charcoal, strapped across the back of the cantle like saddlebags. He lifted them off and turned around.

"Figured all the firewood was damp from the

rain last night. Brought some charcoal and lighter fluid. Don't want to starve to death. Where do I put Salty?" he asked, patting his horse on the neck.

"Foster, Zane, and Daniel put their horses at Kent's house," Jordan answered. "There's still room in with Mac."

We got the fire started and waited for Pepper to come back. As soon as he sat down, I nodded.

Ted jumped to his feet. "Let's go bait the bank poles."

Jordan and I got up, too. "We'll go with you."

At the very same time, all three of us unsnapped, then unzipped our pants. When I nodded, we spun around so our backs were to the rest of the guys and dropped our jeans.

Boos and hisses came from around the campfire.

"That's not fair!" I recognized Foster's voice.

"Yeah," Zane called out. "You guys got on your bathing trunks!"

More boos and hisses filled the air.

Laughing, we turned back to face them.

"You didn't think we were going skinny-dipping again, did you?" Ted chuckled. "How dumb can you be?"

I laughed. "After that catfish attacked me, there's no way I'm getting in the water without *something* on."

That's when I noticed the sly grin on Daniel's face. He nudged Chet in the ribs with his elbow. Both of them stood up. Pepper got to his feet, too.

"Now!" Chet called.

All the other guys unsnapped, unzipped, and spun around to drop their drawers.

Only they had their bathing trunks on, too.

All Jordan, Ted, and I could do was stand there with our mouths gaping open.

Finally we laughed, shook our heads, and laughed some more.

I have to admit, the water felt extra good that evening. I'd spent the whole day working in the heat, helping drag off all those limbs and logs. The lake was cool and relaxing—especially with a bathing suit on.

The three of us worked our way down the line of bank poles. We put worms on the first hook, minnows on the next, and the cut bait that Jordan, Ted, and I had caught on the third. Then we started over again. That way we could keep track of what the catfish were biting on.

At the next to the last pole I stopped.

A weird feeling crept over me—made my muscles tight. Made it hard for me to breathe. I didn't know why. It was kind of like my knees just locked up and I couldn't take another step.

Something was wrong—but for the life of me, I didn't know what it was. Whatever . . . the feeling froze me dead in my tracks.

17

Ted and Jordan were almost to the last pole when they noticed I wasn't with them. They turned. Ted motioned for me to come on. When I still didn't move, they sloshed back.

"What is it, Kent?" Ted frowned. "What's wrong?"

All I could do was stand, chest deep in the water, and shake my head.

"Did something happen?" Jordan asked. "Did you see something?"

Staring toward Mrs. Baum's place, a chill raced up my spine. It started right at my tailbone, scampered up my back, and spread across my shoulders. I rubbed at the little bumps that popped up on my arms.

"Something's just not right," I managed finally. "But . . . but . . . I'm not sure . . . I don't know what."

Both of my friends looked around—all nervous and jumpy—then turned back to me.

"Is this where you first saw the Lake Monster the other night, Kent?" Ted asked.

I shook my head. "No, it was back there," I said, jabbing my thumb over my right shoulder. "Back where the creek comes in."

They scooted closer to each other and yanked their heads around as if looking for something.

"Perhaps this was where you *last* saw the aberration," Jordan suggested.

"The *WHAT*?" Ted yelped.

"Aberration," Jordan repeated.

"Isn't that one of those Australian guys?"

Jordan's lip curled way up on one side. "No, you ditz. You're thinking Aborigine. I said aberration."

Jordan turned to me. Leaning over so he could look me square in the eye, he made sure he had my attention. "Kent, was this where you last saw the *monster*?" He stressed the word *monster* and shot another irritated look at Ted.

I nodded, then pointed. "Yeah. It was right there. Out in the water. I was standing between those two cottonwood . . ."

The word *trees* never came out.

My voice trailed off. My eyes flashed.

That's what it was! That's what was wrong! There was only one big cottonwood tree in front of

Mrs. Baum's place. There had always been two. But . . . now . . .

Once I figured out what was bothering me—what was different—it just took a second to spot where the tree had fallen. A huge ball of dirt-covered roots stood up where the base of the tree used to be. It was bigger around and taller than the three of us put together. The trunk, limbs, and branches were in the lake.

"That's it! The tree. One of the big cottonwood trees must have blown over during the storm."

Wanting to investigate closer, I started toward it. Then I stopped. Be just my luck for Mrs. Baum to be watching. She'd come out and yell at us to get away from her yard. Then she'd stand watch—all night. We never would get to investigate the little shed.

"I see no reason to be apprehensive," Jordan said. "The wind blew a number of trees over. And as for any concerns you might have about the monster . . . You and Zane, both, spotted the aberration late at night. It is doubtful that it would appear this early."

Ted jabbed his fists on both hips and glared at Jordan. "All right! What is it with this *aberration* stuff? Just exactly what does that mean?"

"Well," Jordan began. "It's where, due to your

position or the refraction of light, you see one thing and it appears to be something else. For instance, people on the desert often see a lake where there is none. They see a mirage or an aberration. It's simply heat thermals bending the light so the sand looks like water."

Ted's upper lip curled so high, it almost touched his nose. "What's that got to do with the Lake Monster?"

Jordan heaved a disgusted sigh. "Obviously, there is no such thing as a Lake Monster. Correct?"

Ted nodded.

"Still," Jordan went on, "Zane, Kent, and various other people have seen what *appears* to be the Lake Monster's eyes. Agreed?"

Frowning, Ted nodded again.

"Logically, if there is no such thing as a monster, yet people keep seeing what appears to be a monster—it has to be an aberration. A thing or object that is not what it seems."

Leaving Ted with his mouth gaping open, Jordan turned and started toward the last bank pole. "Of course," he said over his shoulder, "there is a secondary meaning to the word."

"And what's that?" I asked.

"Aberration also means disorder or unsoundness of the mind."

"What?" Ted chimed in.

Jordan's sides jiggled in and out. Even with his back to us, I could tell he was laughing. "Unsoundness of the mind—like, crazy. It means you and Kent are nutty as a fruitcake."

With that, Ted shoved his minnow bucket at me. "Here. Hold this."

Legs churning and hands digging the water, he took off after Jordan. "Crazy? You'll think crazy!"

Jordan heard him coming. Laughing—out loud this time—he sprinted away. They chased and dodged and laughed until I thought they both were going to fall dead in the water from exhaustion. When Ted finally caught him, he grabbed Jordan from behind. He wrapped his arms around Jordan's, pinning them to his sides so he couldn't fight back. Then, lifting with all his might, and leaning to the side, he dunked him. Jordan came up sputtering, but still laughing. Ted dunked him again.

This time, when Ted brought him back up, I saw the strange look on Jordan's face. Eyes wide, he didn't even try to spit the water out. Mouth gaping open, he looked puzzled or scared . . . or something.

Ted threw him under again.

"Stop!" I screamed, racing toward them. "There's something wrong with Jordan!"

I could tell from the look on his face. He'd either swallowed too much water or got choked or . . .

Whatever it was, it was bad!

Ted instantly pulled Jordan back to the surface and loosened his grip. I reached out to help Ted hold him up.

Jordan didn't need help.

He yanked his shoulders back and forth, to get loose. For a moment I thought he was just faking so he could get away.

But once free, he didn't try to run.

Instead he just stood there, frowning down at the water. Then he stuck his head under.

"What is it, Jordan?" I asked when he popped back up. "Are you hurt?"

"Yeah." Ted leaned in from the other side. "What's wrong?"

"SHUT UP!"

Jordan screeched the words so loud, Ted and I kind of jerked back.

I guess the others had heard the commotion, followed by the sudden silence. Flashlights bobbed and bounced down the hill toward us. Jordan stuck his head underwater again. This time Ted and I did the same.

The only thing we could hear were voices and

shouts and splashes. We looked up. The guys raced out in the lake to see what we were doing.

"Everybody *STOP!*" Jordan barked. "Stand real still and put your head under the water. Don't say anything, just listen."

Daniel kind of sneered at him. But when everyone else did what Jordan told them to . . .

At first I didn't hear a thing. Then faint—far away—I heard it.

Tap, tap, tap. A long pause. *Tap . . . tap . . . tap.* Another long pause, followed by three more quick taps.

All of us snapped our heads up about the same time.

"What is it, Jordan?" Foster wondered. "What's going on?"

"Somebody's in trouble," he barked. "They need help."

Daniel, our fearless leader, folded his arms. His lip curled up on one side.

"That's bull. It's just somebody tapping on something. Jordan—the nerd—is flippin' out again."

Jordan turned to glare at him. "Three short, three long, three short. It's an SOS. It's Morse code, you moron! A distress signal."

Daniel bristled up like a porcupine. His sunken

chin sloped so sharply toward his neck, it looked like he was about to swallow it. "I'm the general of this outfit! Nobody calls me a moron," he snarled. "I'm gonna beat the snot out of . . ." Fists doubled, he charged toward Jordan.

I jumped between them and tried to stop Daniel. He took a swing at me, but I ducked. Then Pepper was there, holding him. Chet jumped in to help Pepper.

"I'll get both of you," Daniel threatened as they walked him to the bank. "I'll tear both of you to shreds."

Jordan ignored him and started talking to Ted about how they could home in on the sound. I pretended to ignore Daniel, too. He was popular at school and a good athlete, but there was still something kind of sneaky about him. Especially when he was mad. I felt like I needed to keep an eye on him.

Daniel paced up and down the bank, glaring out into the lake at Jordan and me. After a while he even climbed up on the trunk of the fallen tree and stomped around. It was like he was trying to get closer to us. Sort of reminded me of a cat waiting for the opportunity to pounce on a mouse.

"Kent?"

The sound of my name turned my attention back to Jordan. "What?"

"I'll need your mask and snorkel," Jordan said. "We also need something metal, like a couple of wrenches or something so I can communicate with this guy. Try to find out where he is and . . ."

Suddenly an ear-piercing scream shattered the night air. It made us jump. Sent the chills racing all over me.

For an instant I thought it was Mrs. Baum. She must have finally spotted us, really close to her front yard, and was yelling at us to get off her property.

I froze in my tracks.

"The *MONSTER!*" The scream came again. "It's here! It's right here!"

Frantic eyes darted about. I finally spotted Daniel, out on the fallen cottonwood tree. He jumped up and down a couple of times, pointing at the water. Then he spun to race back up the trunk toward shore.

Only he turned too quick. His foot slipped.

Arms flailing—spinning round and round like the blades of a helicopter—he swayed one way, then the other. Finally he toppled over. Crashed through the branches and splashed into the lake.

Out of sight for an instant, he finally fought his way to the surface. He yelled again:

"It's the monster! It's got my leg! *Help!*"

18

Panic does funny things to a person. Here Daniel was—in trouble—screaming and flopping around in the lake. He needed help.

The rest of us took off. We were a good twenty yards up the hill before we stopped. I don't even remember running. I was just there, panting for air and looking over my shoulder. All seven of us were clumped together like a covey of quail. Trembling and shaking, we reached to our sides and behind us, searching for someone to cling to.

And just as quickly as the unexpected scream had sent me running for the hill, I spun and raced back.

Panic is the most dangerous thing in the world when someone is in the water. I'd been to enough water-safety courses with Dad to know that. Most times—even being trapped underwater and running out of air in a scuba tank—a person could survive. He could get free, save his life, just as long as he kept his cool. Just as long as he stayed calm.

Daniel was *not* calm!

As I ran toward him, all I could see were his face and hands. Fingernails dug at the bark of the cottonwood as he tried to pull himself up. Face barely above the surface, he kept yanking and tugging. Fighting for his life.

I leaped to the trunk of the tree. It was wide and so heavy in the water, there was no spring or bounce. I ran along the length, squeezed past one huge branch, and hopped around a smaller one. Finally I was right over him.

I'd never seen such a pitiful, terrified, helpless look on anyone's face in my life. Daniel was always the leader—the take-charge guy. But not now. Eyes wide and filled with tears, he reached up to me.

"It's got my leg! It's trying to pull me under. Help me! Please . . . please . . ."

I dropped to one knee and reached out an arm.

But before Daniel could grab for me, I yanked my hand back and scrambled to my feet.

"When you're in the water, never let someone in a panic get hold of you. They'll take you under with them and you'll both drown." Dad's words echoed in my ears as if he were standing right beside me.

I looked around for a long stick or broken branch. Something I could hold out for him to grab. Daniel slipped under the surface once more. He came up sputtering and coughing.

"The monster . . . Help me, Kent!" he begged.

Fingertips clawing at the tree bark, he pulled up, then let go with one hand and reached out to me.

A sudden smile tugged at the corners of my mouth. Each time Daniel kicked and struggled, a little clump of leaves, about three yards behind him, sloshed and splashed the water.

"Daniel, you're hung on a tree limb. It's not the monster. Just relax."

His eyes were wide and frantic. "It's got my leg! It's trying to drag me away. Help—please!"

"It's a tree limb, Daniel!"

He didn't hear a word I said. I looked around. Behind me the others had worked their way, cautious and slow, to the base of the fallen tree.

"Kent . . . don't let it eat me," he whimpered. "I don't want to die."

Once more he lunged and jerked. Loosing his grip on the tree, he went under. Bark ripped beneath his fingers as he violently clawed his way back to the surface. The leaves behind him splashed and bobbed.

I dropped to my stomach on the log. Quick as a cat—so he wouldn't have a chance to grab my arm—I reached out and bopped him on the head. He didn't even notice. So . . . I hit him again. Harder this time.

Daniel's eyes flashed. He blinked a couple of times and looked up at me.

"It's a tree limb." I spoke softly. "Quit yanking."

"But . . . but . . ."

"Be still. You're tangled up in a branch. I'll get you out, but quit crying and jumping around. Just hold on a second."

Once calm, I had Daniel hold on to my arm. Then I told him to feel around with his other foot to see if he could tell how he was stuck.

"Okay," he said finally. "There's a *V* or a fork over the front of my right foot."

"Can you slide your foot back?"

Daniel shook his head. "No. There's another branch behind it. It's really stuck."

I felt his fingers tighten around my wrist.

"Okay. Calm down. Slide your left foot behind your ankle. See if you can wedge your toes in there and shove the branch off. If not, try to push it far enough so you can wiggle your heel out."

His grip tightened even more. I grabbed his wrist with both hands. Suddenly Daniel's eyes flashed wide. Without a word of warning, he grabbed my elbow with his free hand. Then my shoulder, and finally a fistful of my hair as he climbed his way up me to get out of the water.

I felt like I'd been in a fight with a bobcat or

something. I was scratched and clawed and probably bleeding.

Never stopping to say so much as thank you, Daniel climbed over me. Staying on all fours, he crawled down the log and hopped onto the shore. By the time I got back to them, they had already asked Daniel about seeing the monster.

"Bubbles?" Chet's head tilted to one side and he let out a little laugh. "All that over some bubbles? That's as bad as Kent's wild catfish attack."

Everyone started laughing. Only instead of laughing with them, like I did when the catfish scared me, Daniel got mad. No longer crying, he puffed his chest out and pushed his shoulders back.

"Not just bubbles," he snapped, trying to take charge again. "I've seen bubbles from turtles or little pockets of air oozing up from the mud. These bubbles were huge. It was like . . . like somebody had flushed a giant toilet. Just a big *baloosh*!"

"Like air coming from a scuba tank?" Pepper frowned.

Daniel shook his head. "No. Bigger. Lots bigger."

Jordan left us and walked out on the log. He stood, staring down at the water, then raced back. "It's right there!" he yelped. "Right under the tree.

I could hear it, even without putting my head under the water." He turned to me. "I need your mask and snorkel."

I shook my head. "You can't see down there. Not after the rain and at night."

"Don't need to see," Jordan said. "Just have to keep my head under long enough to communicate." He turned to Ted. "Go up to Mrs. Baum's and see if she'll give you a couple of wrenches or something. I need two pieces of metal I can clank together so I can send Morse code."

I sprinted for home.

Ted and I got back about the same time. I handed Jordan the snorkel and mask. Ted handed him two large rusty wrenches.

"Mrs. Baum wasn't home. That's why it took me so long," he explained. "But Dad and I helped clean her barn out last summer. I remembered seeing these, so I just went and got them."

Jordan put the mask and snorkel on. Holding the wrenches, he walked out on the log, found a big limb that was lying in the water, and draped himself over it. It looked kind of weird. His legs dangled down on one side and his head and arms dangled down on the other. All we could see was his rear end sticking up in the air.

We waited. And waited. Finally Jordan came

back and stood on the base of the log, looking down at us.

"Okay. We need help. There's some guy trapped in a submarine. I think the tree fell on him or something. He's running out of air and can't get out."

There was total silence. I guess everybody else was thinking the same thing I was.

Submarine?

In Cedar Lake?

We stared at Jordan. No one breathed. No one blinked. We just stared.

The silence grew and grew. No waves lapped the shore. No crickets chirped in the grass.

Just silence.

19

Daniel's laugh finally broke the silence. It wasn't a fun laugh. It was one of those dirty, ugly laughs that irritated the night stillness like a pesky mosquito humming in your ear.

"Submarine in Cedar Lake. Ha! That's the most ridiculous thing I ever heard. What are you trying to pull?"

Daniel made a complete turnaround from the scared little kid with tears rolling down his cheeks. He didn't even act like the same guy that I had saved only moments earlier. Arms folded and eyes narrowed, he got right in Jordan's face.

Jordan sighed and raised his finger to the bridge of his nose so he could push his glasses up. Then he remembered he didn't have any glasses on, so he sighed again.

"Okay. I tapped out two short, two long, and two short. That's Morse code for *question*. You know, a question mark . . ."

"And?" Daniel snipped, still not believing a word Jordan said.

"And . . . they tapped back three short—the letter *s*, two shorts and one long—the letter *u*, followed by a long and three shorts—the letter *b*. In other words—*sub*. Then I tapped—"

"Wait a minute, Jordan," I said, cutting him off. "We don't have time to learn that code stuff right now. Just tell us what they said."

"Oh." He shrugged. "Okay. They said, 'Sub. Trapped. Need air.'"

All we could do was stand there. The silence swept in again. We stared at Jordan. Stared at the lake, then stared back at Jordan again.

"There's no way someone could get a submarine in Cedar Lake," Pepper scoffed. "Those things are huge."

Chet shook his head. "Not necessarily. Some submersibles are quite small. Why, even back in World War II, the Japanese were using two-man subs to spy on Honolulu and—"

"And . . ." Jordan cut in, "I was doing some research the other day on the Cayman Islands. They have these two- or three-man submersibles that can dive to over three thousand feet. They're really heavy, but they're relatively small, compared to what we normally think of as a submarine."

Foster waved his hands. "Okay, so there are

small submarines. But . . . but why in Cedar Lake?"

No one—not even Jordan—had an answer to that one.

Ted turned and started up the hill. "Look, it doesn't matter. Someone is trapped down there, in something. They're trapped, running out of air, and we have to help them. Come on, Kent."

I headed up the hill—but Ted went left and I went right. "Where you going?" he called.

"Mrs. Baum's. It's closer."

"She's not home."

I frowned. "Are you sure?"

"When I went after the wrenches for Jordan, I pounded on both doors until my hand hurt. She's not home."

We jogged to my house to call. I didn't have the nerve to tell the dispatcher that there was a submarine in Cedar Lake. I simply said there was someone trapped underwater and we needed the Emergency Rescue Unit. The man on the phone could tell I was a kid, and he started questioning me. When I told him who I was, he knew Dad, he knew he was at a wedding shower at the church, and he said he'd notify him, too.

"Be sure and tell him that I'm fine. And none of us kids is hurt or in trouble. Otherwise, he'll flip out."

The dispatcher promised he would.

The summer after we first moved here, Mom and Dad had a big picnic and invited a whole bunch of the firefighters who Dad worked with. Since most of the guys knew where we lived, our driveway is where we decided to wait.

I saw the lights before I ever heard the siren.

Blue, yellow, and red flashed and streaked across the dam so fast that the EMS truck was almost to the middle before the sound reached me. At the corner of the dam, I lost sight of them for a moment. Then they were on our road, headed straight for me.

The EMS truck slowed. Then I guess when they saw me waving in their headlights, they sped up and slid to a stop right beside where Ted and I stood.

"Hey, squirt," a familiar voice greeted. "How's my old fishin' buddy?"

It was Greg Ratcliff. Greg was one of Dad's fishing buddies. He was fun and I liked it when he came to the house or when Dad let me go fishing with the two of them. Pete Barsto drove the truck. He leaned around Greg and nodded. Pete was a short, stocky young man with dark skin and brown eyes. He was nice, too, only he wasn't as much fun as Greg.

Arms dangling over the passenger-side doorway, Greg reached out and ruffled my hair. "Hear you got a problem. Where we supposed to be?"

Ted and I hopped on the running boards on either side of the truck. Pete drove slowly, until we got to the gate that opened into the vacant lot. There, I hopped off and pointed toward the lake. "The water's about sixty yards down that way. The tree's about twenty yards left of the fence line, here. You'll see the guys standing around. That's where it is."

"Don't want to get stuck or lose the light trailer we're pulling. Any ravines or creeks to fall into?"

"I don't think so."

Greg glanced to the other side, where Ted was hanging on. "Son, why don't you and I walk in front. We'll watch for drop-offs, and Kent can wait here for his father."

"Dad's coming?"

"Not more than five minutes behind us. We'll go ahead and set up, okay, squirt?"

"Sure, Greg."

I watched them drive down the hill and stop. When I glanced back to the dam, three more sets of headlights were racing across. They weren't going as fast as the EMS unit had, but almost.

Greg and Pete already had the light trailer

unhooked and set up by the time Dad and the other fathers arrived. I rode down with Dad and Mr. Aikman.

Snorkel and mask in hand, Pete walked toward the lake. Greg was still trying to get the lights on. There was a long pole on one side of the trailer with a bank of about five enormous floodlights. They had raised the pole and locked it in place, then extended the telescoping part until the lights were about fifteen feet up in the air. Greg pulled on this cord, over and over again, as if starting a lawnmower. Finally the generator coughed and sputtered a couple of times. He pulled again and it settled to a smooth almost quiet hum. Once it was running, he turned the lights on.

Suddenly it was bright as day.

After parking their cars out of the way, the other men came pouring out, trying to find their sons. Chet was out on the fallen tree. Foster, Daniel, Ted, Pepper, and Zane stood near the clump of dirt-covered roots at the base. When the lights came on, they flinched and quickly raised a hand to shelter their eyes from the bright glare. The dads, who stood right beside me, kind of surged forward. Necks stretched and standing on their tiptoes, each searched for his son. One at a time they seemed to relax. All but Jordan's dad.

"Jordan? Where are you? Jordan?"

As bright as it was, I already had Jordan spotted. Chet crouched on the tree trunk, right where the branches were under the water. Jordan was lying across one of the bigger limbs. All I could see was his back and the tip of my snorkel. When Chet tapped his leg, he brought his head up and looked around. Then Chet said something to him. Jordan pulled the mask off and got to his knees.

"I'm down here, Dad. I'm fine. But you need to tell the rescue people to hurry."

We headed down to the shore. About the time we got there, Pete Barsto raised his head above water.

"Greg," he called. "They're right. There's somebody down here. When Simon gets here, have him—"

"I'm here, Pete!" Dad called.

"Good, Simon. Let's get our stuff on. We'll have to go take a look. Oh . . . need the lights, too."

Pete Barsto was quite a bit younger than Dad. He didn't jog to the truck, he sprinted. We heard the door fly open, and in just a matter of seconds both men were out of their clothes and into their wet suits. Gear in hand, they trotted to the edge of the lake. Then they waded out into the water and then . . .

They were gone.

The only thing left was a swirl of water, glistening in the glow of the big floodlights.

I held my breath, watching. In the daylight I could always find a bubble trail—bubbles coming up whenever someone exhales. In the dark I couldn't see a thing. I didn't like Dad being out of my sight. I didn't like him diving in the dark. Hardly realizing how long I'd been holding my breath, the air made a big poof sound when I let it out and sucked in a new one.

Then I started pacing.

Dad paced, sometimes, when he was really nervous. I never did.

"He's okay," I whispered to myself when I was away from the others. "He's been with the fire department for a long time. He's done lots of underwater rescues. Well, not lots, but some. And . . . and . . . there are tree limbs and probably barbed wire and hard telling what else down there. And . . . and . . . it's night. It's dark."

The word *dark* hung in my throat. And when it came out, it hung in the night air like an unseen spider's web.

20

When Dad and Pete Barsto surfaced and swam into shore, it was like an unspoken signal for us to rush closer and see what was going on. We were all careful not to crowd them or get in the way. At the same time everyone simply *had to be* close enough to hear what was said.

"Submarine," Dad said.

There was no expression to his voice. Just the word. He didn't even look at us. He just stared down at the ground and shook his head. Finally he glanced up at Pete Barsto. "Submarine?"

Pete nodded. "That's what I saw." He shrugged. "Thing's about nine feet long," he explained to us. "Teardrop shaped. Wheel-operated hatch on the top. About five feet in diameter and tapers to a propeller with a guard around it at the back." He looked at Dad. "Did you see anybody inside?"

Dad shook his head. "There's a small glass view port. Too many tree limbs, though. I couldn't get close enough to look inside."

Jordan and Greg had come down the log to listen, too.

"Any way we can pull it out?" Greg asked.

Dad cleared his throat.

"Pinned under the limbs of that cottonwood. Doesn't appear to be any damage to it—but it's stuck, that's for sure."

"Maybe we could pull the tree off," Greg suggested.

"No way," Pete said with a quick shake of his head. "That thing is enormous. Take three wreckers to budge that tree." He folded his lips inside his mouth and nibbled on them. "Maybe if we cut some of the bigger branches off, we could get it loose."

Dad folded his arms and shot a blast of air up his forehead.

"That won't work. The big limbs that have the thing pinned are on the underside of the tree. Can't cut underwater."

As they kept discussing what to do, the rest of us sort of inched closer. I noticed Foster wasn't quite with the group. He stood over to the side, looking at the big tree in the water. Then he stared up at the other cottonwood tree, the one that was still standing. Then back down at the water again.

"Mr. Morgan," he called. "Exactly where is the sub?"

Dad pointed. "Little to the right of center, about twenty-five feet out."

"Kind of where most of the branches are?"

"Yeah."

Foster scratched his chin.

"How about if you cut a couple of the bigger limbs off—the ones you can reach with the saw. Then cut the trunk. About where it goes underwater." He pointed down at the enormous tree. "Most of the weight is in the trunk. You cut the top off, maybe you could move that."

Head tilted to one side, Dad smiled. He whipped around and studied the tree for a moment.

"Kid's pretty darned sharp," he said. "Let Pete and me go down and take another look. Maybe we have a couple of big branches, up toward the bank, that aren't holding the sub down. If we left them, it would take enough pressure off so we could cut through the trunk. Then we could either pull the top of the tree off the thing or at least roll it off."

Dad and Pete put their masks on, stuffed their hoses in their mouths, and sloshed back into the lake. Greg already had the chain saw out of the truck before they came back to the surface. It looked a lot like our chain saw, only the thing was bigger and the blade was over three times as long.

"Leave this big one," Dad called, when he came back to the surface.

Greg nodded.

"And these two." Pete slapped a couple of limbs on the other side of the trunk. "They're solid enough to help support the tree and not in the way."

"Get all the branches you can reach," Dad said. "Got to get some weight off this end. Pete and I will drag them out of the way for you."

Greg pulled more times on the chain saw than he had to on the light generator. It finally kicked in, and he walked out to start cutting. As he cut off limbs, Dad or Pete would take them and swim toward the bank. After about the second limb, Mr. Aikman gave a little snort.

"This is going to take forever," he said. "They need some help."

With that, he strolled down the bank about twenty yards and started pulling his shoes and socks off. The other dads followed.

If we hadn't been so worried about the poor guy who was trapped in the submarine, we would have probably burst out laughing when they came back. We had on our bathing trunks. The fathers—who had just come from a fancy dinner party dressed in suits and ties—had stripped down to their underwear. Boxers with wild colors and designs, and two pairs of jockey shorts, waded in and out of the water, helping drag the branches away.

We pitched in, too.

Greg worked on the tree until he was standing knee deep, way out on the log. Except for the very tip, most of the branches that were sticking above the water were gone. He then came back to a spot on the trunk where the top of the log met the water, and started cutting.

It took a lot longer to saw through the enormous trunk than it did to get the limbs off. As the blade spun, water sprayed in the air like a rooster tail from a Wave Runner. The water danced and sparkled in the glow of the spotlights. Dad told us that as long as the motor and the exhaust were out of the water, it shouldn't drown out.

All at once he kind of lunged forward. Almost falling over headfirst, he managed to catch himself before he went into the lake. The saw sputtered, coughed, then died.

"We're through," he called.

Everyone on the bank cheered. Dad picked up his scuba gear. Pete looked around for his.

"All I have to do is tie the cable on, Pete. I can do that by myself."

"Go ahead." Pete nodded. "I'll get the EMS unit lined up, and the winch line strung out. Figure as damp as this ground is, I may have to move the truck up the hill a couple of times. We got plenty of cable, though." He scurried off toward the truck.

"Kent," Dad called. "Go up and tell Mrs. Baum what we're doing down here. If she looks out her window and sees that truck in her front yard, it's liable to scare her half to death."

"She's not home, Dad," I called back.

Dad frowned. "What do you mean she's not home? It's after nine."

"We tried to call from her house when Jordan first heard the SOS," Ted answered. "She's not there."

Dad gave a little laugh. "She's probably sleeping. Rowdy, you mind going with them? See if you can get her up."

Mr. Aikman nodded. He went to the pile of clothes on the bank and slipped his trousers on. Then he motioned Ted and me to follow.

"Told you so." Ted smiled after we'd circled the house twice and pounded on every door and window.

Mr. Aikman shot him a look, then turned

back to stare at Mrs. Baum's front door.

"It just doesn't make sense," he said, more to himself than to us. "She doesn't spend the night with friends. There are no kids or grandchildren for her to go visit. She's got to be in there."

He jiggled the doorknob again. "Something is wrong." There was a tightness in his voice. Worry. "Maybe she's fallen or had a heart attack or . . . I'm going in!"

With that, he lunged. There was a cracking sound when his shoulder and hip slammed against the wooden door. I jumped. Eyes wide, Ted and I both stepped back. When it didn't open, he threw himself at it again.

21

Rowdy Aikman threw his shoulder against the door three more times before it gave. He made us stay on the front porch. I guess he was afraid of what he might find. After searching through the whole house, he came back.

"Things always look easier on TV than in real life," he said, rubbing his sore shoulder. "It just doesn't make sense."

"The other night I was up here," I confessed. "She was doing something in the work shed. Maybe she's there."

Mr. Aikman glanced down the hill and, with a jerk of his head, motioned us to follow. Pete already had the truck at the far edge of Mrs. Baum's front yard. When I saw it sitting there, a little chill scampered up my back. Inside my skull I could almost hear that shrill voice: "You boys get out of my yard." The sound never came to my ears, though.

There was no way that Mrs. Baum was around. She had a built-in sense—almost like radar or something—that went off if anyone came in her front yard. No matter what she was doing or where she was, if she saw that truck, she'd be here, yelling.

As we stepped from the porch, I could see Pete and Greg staring down into the water. They waited for Dad to attach the cable. When he surfaced and started for the shore, Greg joined the rest of the men and moved them back. Pete trotted to the truck.

About halfway to the work shed, we stopped walking a moment and watched when we heard the winch whining. Nothing happened. It changed pitch, and still no movement came from the tree limbs. Pete appeared from the back of the truck and climbed into the cab. He inched it forward. After only a foot or so, the wheels began to spin. Grass and little bits of dirt flew up. He raced the motor. The truck slipped toward the lake, just a bit.

Pete climbed out and pulled more cable. Back in the truck, he let it roll back, to get out of the shallow ruts. Then he drove forward, slow and easy until the cable was taunt. This time when he drove forward, we saw the big limb where Dad had attached the cable rise up out of the water.

We held our breath. Watched. The limb came partly above the surface. I felt my fists clench at my sides. Just a few more feet and the whole top part of the tree would roll and . . .

Then the spinning, whizzing sound of tires slipping on grass and mud came to our ears again. While Pete hopped out to release more cable, we got to the work shed. Mr. Aikman knocked on the door. An open lock dangled and bounced against the wood when he pounded.

"Emma? Are you in here? This is Rowdy. Emma?"

Mr. Aikman opened the door. The old hinges squeaked. Facing the lake, the work shed was downhill from the light generator. It was dark as pitch inside. I could hear his fingers patting the wall as he felt for the light switch.

When the lights came on, he started inside. But he stepped back instead—kind of straightened like a soldier snapping to attention.

"My gosh." He breathed. "What in the world . . ."

Ted and I moved to the sides, trying to see past him. He leaned forward and peeked one way, then the other, before he finally stepped inside.

The floor was concrete. That was about all we could see at first. But when he moved farther, we saw part of the far wall. There were about five long shelves that stretched the entire length of the shed. The shelves were lined with small square boxes—

like batteries—and there were all sorts of cables running back and forth. Looking from side to side, Mr. Aikman took another step or two.

Suddenly he stopped and kind of staggered backward.

"What . . . what . . ." he stammered, looking down at the floor. "I don't believe this!"

Ted and I tried to squeeze through the door at the same time. Our shoulders wedged against the side. We glared at each other, then wiggled free and sort of popped on through.

The walls to our left and right were lined with shelves, too. There were more batteries and more wires and more cables. Then we looked down where Mr. Aikman was staring.

The work shed was about fifteen feet square. Only I could tell, from the first look inside, it *wasn't* a work shed.

Right in the center was a big, gaping dark hole. Ted and I kind of jammed on our brakes and slipped into reverse. Except for the shelves with the batteries, that's mostly what the entire room was. A cover built over this huge hole. Of the fifteen-foot square room, the hole took up about ten square feet of floor space. There was barely enough concrete around the edges to get to the shelves. The rest of it was dark and empty.

Sliding out a foot for balance, I leaned forward. The far side of the hole—the one I could see—had a concrete wall. I still couldn't see the bottom. Again I scooted forward. The walls of the hole, on my left and right, were concrete. Still no bottom to the thing.

I'd heard of "bottomless pits." I'd never seen one. My knees trembled when I took another step.

A good twelve feet down, there was water. A line of pale green moss lined the edges—staining where the water met the concrete. Right under my feet was a steel ladder that went down, to disappear beneath the surface. The water seemed clear. Not murky and cloudy like the lake. Even with the clear water and the bright lights above us in the shed, I couldn't see the bottom—couldn't tell how deep it was.

Standing just next to me on my left, Mr. Aikman squatted down. He put his left hand on the ground for balance, then leaned so he could look at something to our right.

The concrete I had seen there only went down about a foot. Then it stopped. The hole, along with the water in the bottom of it, continued—toward the lake—and disappeared into the blackness.

"What is that, Dad?" Ted asked. "It looks like a cave or tunnel. Why is it here?"

I glanced at Mr. Aikman. His eyes were wide. He sprang to his feet.

"Move!" he barked. "Get out of the way!"

Ted and I scrambled, almost toppling over each other, as we tried to scoot out of his path. He raced through the doorway. We clambered to our feet to follow.

Waving his arms, he ran toward the truck.

"Stop!" he screamed at the top of his lungs. "Pete! Stop!"

Almost in a direct line between us and the lake, the truck's motor roared. Tires slipped and spun for an instant, then caught and moved the truck forward again. A quick glance let my eyes follow the cable toward the lake. It was tight enough to play a tune on. Then I could see the big limb rise above the surface as the entire top of the tree rolled from its resting place.

The Emergency Rescue Unit surged forward.

A muffled but loud *crack* exploded above the roar of the motor.

The front of the truck went down. The rear end went up. A high-pitched whizzing sound came when the back wheels left the ground. In the blink of an eye the whole thing disappeared—as if swallowed up by the earth—and all I could see was the rear end, the winch, and the cable.

22

I never knew old guys could move so fast. Everyone raced from the lake to see what had happened. The men got there first. They even beat Ted and me. And we were closer.

Greg Ratcliff had a flashlight snapped to his belt. He dropped to one knee and shined it down the driver's side of the truck.

I could hear him yelling for Pete, but I didn't hear an answer—not until we got closer.

"I'm fine," Pete called back. "I'm okay."

Greg shined the light. Dad knelt down next to him.

"What happened?" Pete shouted again. "What did I drive into?"

"Some kind of trench," Greg said.

"Tunnel," Dad corrected. "Walls are concrete. Bridge timbers over the top, covered with dirt and grass roots. They're so old and rotten, they couldn't hold the truck. Can you open the door?"

"No."

"Is it jammed or stuck?"

There was a long silence, then a little laugh. An almost uncomfortable chuckle.

"Okay . . . it's not stuck, but . . . well . . . I guess I'm not all right, after all. Think my left arm is broken."

Dad climbed down into the tunnel with Pete, while Greg went for a ladder out of the back of the truck.

"It's broke, all right." I overheard him yell. "Arm's flopping around like a wet noodle."

Once they had Pete out, they made him sit down on the ground. Dad and Greg climbed into the back of the EMS truck to get a splint for his arm. Resting on its nose, the big doors wouldn't stay open. Jordan's dad and Chet's dad had to hold them. Finding the splints was a little tricky, too. When the truck tipped, everything must have fallen from its normal storage place and piled up near the front of the truck. I could hear Dad and Greg digging around, trying to find things.

"Why in the world is there a trench out in the middle of nowhere?" Mr. Hamilton asked, shining the light down beside the truck.

"Don't know," Mr. Aikman answered. "I do know that it goes from the lake up to Mrs. Baum's work shed."

"Only, it's not a work shed," I chimed in. "It's a boathouse."

The bright light from the flashlight made me squeeze my eyes tight.

It's funny how clear things can be in the dark, sometimes. With my eyes shut—with all the noise and commotion—with all the worry about Pete and his broken arm—with all the discussion about what to do next, now that the truck was stuck . . . well . . . everything was suddenly as clear as could be.

"Mrs. Baum," I breathed.

I guess I whispered her name so softly that no one heard me but Ted. He was the only one close enough.

"Huh?" he asked.

"Mrs. Baum," I repeated.

The whole crowd looked at me like I was as dumb as dirt.

Ted shook his head. "She's not home, remember?"

I pointed to the lake. "No, it's Mrs. Baum."

"What about Mrs. Baum?"

"She's the Monster of Cedar Lake. She's the one trapped in the submarine."

I knew it all along, probably. Only I just didn't *know* that I knew.

"Kent," Ted said. "You're losin' it. What are you talking about?"

I didn't answer. I just stared off into the dark.

It all made sense now. People were always talking about seeing the monster's eyes, but no one ever saw the monster. The first time I saw them— that night with Zane at our first fishing trip—the eyes were yellow or orange. The night I was alone they were white-hot.

Headlights.

Headlights were white. Except when the battery was low. (I remember when Mom left the lights on one night. When I got up to go to school the next day, they were yellow and kind of sickly looking.) The eyes were headlights.

A work shed that wasn't a work shed. There were no tools, just batteries and cables to keep them charged. The submarine, as well as the lights, probably worked off batteries.

The night I sneaked out of the house, the eyes came toward me as I stood on the bank. Shaking and scared, I knew that any moment the monster was going to slosh out of the water and come after me. Only it didn't. In water that should have been two to three feet deep, it simply vanished.

The tunnel.

Then Mrs. Baum screamed at me and almost made me pee my pants.

It had to be her!

"KENT!"

I jumped when Ted roared my name.

Blinking a few times, I looked around. Except for Dad and Greg, who were busy putting the splint on Pete's broken arm, the whole group stood staring at me with open mouths.

Ted waved a hand in front of my face. "You okay, Kent? You were spaced out or something, there for a while. What happened? It was like you just went off and left us—you know, like Jordan does. What . . ."

Ted flinched. He clamped his lips closed, suddenly realizing Mr. Parks was standing right beside him. Looking up with a sheepish smile, he gave a little shrug.

"Sorry, Mr. Parks. No offense."

Mr. Parks smiled down at him. "None taken. I know how Jordan is."

They turned back to me.

"What were you talking about, Kent?" Ted finished what he was trying to say.

While I explained the whole thing to them, Dad climbed down the ladder to use the EMS radio in the truck and call for another ambulance.

I was just finishing up when he came out of the

trench. "It'll be about thirty minutes!" he called to Pete and Greg. "They're on another call."

"We don't have thirty minutes!"

It was Jordan's voice, but he wasn't standing with the rest of us. Even when he was with us, most times he wasn't *really* with us. Guess that's why no one noticed he was missing. When he called, we all turned toward the voice.

Water dripped from his bathing suit. Shoulders sagging, he still carried the two big wrenches in his hands as he sloshed toward us from the lake.

"What do you mean, 'we don't have thirty minutes'?" Dad called.

"When the top of the tree rolled, everyone came running up here to see what happened. I went out and told the guy"—he lifted a wrench—"to try and move the sub."

"And?" Dad urged.

"And the tapping was so light I could barely hear it. You know, really weak. All I got back was three letters. N. O. A."

Everyone stood there. Puzzled. Staring at Jordan.

Suddenly there was a little yelp when Pete struggled to get to his feet. Greg tried to make him sit back on the ground, but Pete shoved him aside with his good arm.

"Kid's right," he said. "N. O. A. No a. No *air*. That's what she was trying to say, only she's too weak to finish it. We don't have time to wait on the other unit. We've got to do something—now!"

23

One handed, Pete managed to fight Greg and Dad off. He kept telling them that his arm wasn't hurting and that he *wasn't* going into shock. They finally listened, and we all followed Pete and Jordan down to the water.

That didn't help Mrs. Baum much, because all we did once we got there was stand and stare.

"We could use one of the pickups," Mr. Bently suggested finally. "Take the cable off the EMS thing. Attach it to a pickup and—"

"No way," Greg said, shaking his head. "That's a two-ton truck with mud-grip tires. It could barely move the tree limb. Pickups don't have enough weight, and the tires don't have enough traction. All the thing would do is sit and spin."

"How about if we all got hold of the cable and pulled?" Mr. Hamilton said. "Counting the boys, there's sixteen of us here. That might give us enough weight to haul the thing up."

This time Dad shook his head.

"No way to get a grip on that quarter-inch steel

cable." He sighed. "Besides, I don't think sixteen of us could move it."

"You've got a scuba tank with air," Mr. Shift said. "Now that the tree's off it, maybe you could open the hatch and—"

Pete cut him off. "That's always a last resort. Way the water rushes in, most times you can't get air to them fast enough. Even a young person— healthy and strong—has a sixty percent chance of drowning. Chances of reviving them with CPR— especially someone as old as Mrs. Baum—well, her chances would be almost zero."

Again we fell to silence and stood to stare out at the lake. Time was running out—and quick. We had to do something . . . but there was nothing we could do except wait for the other EMS truck. That would be at least another twenty-five minutes. There was just nothing . . .

"Horses!"

The way I blurted out the word startled everyone. Even me. We all jumped.

"We could use the horses," I repeated. "We've got a bunch of rope lying around in the garage. Their hooves can get traction, even in the mud— you know, where a truck tire can't. They're strong, too. Plenty strong enough."

"I . . . I don't . . . know," Dad hesitated. "We've

got a bunch of rope up there, but it might not be enough."

"There's rope in Mrs. Baum's hay barn, up behind the house," Mr. Aikman said. "Ted and I cleaned the barn out for her last spring. Some of it's kind of old, but . . ."

"We've got three lariats in Jordan's horse barn," Mr. Parks spoke up.

"The steel guard around the propeller looked strong enough," Pete said. "We could tie on to that. Should work." When no one said anything or did anything, Pete waved his good arm at us. "Well, quit standing around talking. *Move!*"

Dad nodded. "Boys! Get your horses. Make sure the saddles are cinched up tight. Greg—come with me to carry the rope from my garage. Rowdy, you go to the hay barn." He looked around for Jordan's dad. Mr. Parks didn't wait for instructions. Already past the light generator, all we could see of him were his white boxers, bobbing in the moonlight.

Even with nothing on but our bathing trunks, and running around in the dark, it still took us only five to ten minutes to get the horses saddled and ride them back to the base of the big cotton-wood. Dad and Greg were the last to come back. That's because the pile of ropes each of them carried was so big they had trouble lugging it around.

The fire department used lots of rope. Each year they bought new, and the firefighters could purchase the used ropes from the city. Guess Dad had been collecting it for quite a while. "Rope is like duct tape," he'd say, when Mom complained about the collection in the barn. "Never can have too much."

Dad went to get his scuba gear on while the men began straightening the ropes. We helped them by unrolling the different lengths and checking for knots. If the ropes were too short to reach, Mr. Aikman or Greg tied two together. Once that was done, they inspected them again, threw out the ropes that seemed old or weak, and replaced them with better ones.

When all was said and done, we had eight strands of rope—each about thirty to forty feet long—stretched out in eight lines. The lines gathered near the base of the tree and spread out like a fan, going up the hill.

Leading our horses, we joined the men near the fallen tree. That's when I noticed Pete struggling with one arm to get his tank on. Dad stopped him. "You're not going down."

Pete kind of crinkled his nose. "Why not? Take you forever to tie those ropes on. Least I can do is hold the light for you."

"You've got a broken arm."

"It's in a plastic blow-up splint. Water's not gonna bother it."

"No."

"You're not diving alone. That's the first thing they ever taught us—you never dive alone."

"It's not that deep," Dad argued. "There are no currents. Now that the tree's out of the way, there are no obstructions or anything to get caught on. It's a safe dive. Easy."

One of Pete's eyebrows arched so high, it almost disappeared into his hairline. "And just how do you plan to tie ropes and hold an underwater light?"

"Well, I'll . . . I'll . . ."

"Can't be done, Simon. You've got to have help down there."

"How about Greg?" one of the men suggested.

Greg kind of ducked his head.

Dad smiled. "I was with that man about three years ago. Saw him run into a blazing house to find a kid. Bravest man I ever met. But when it comes to water . . ." Dad's voice trailed off and he shook his head.

Mr. Shift puffed his chest out and stepped forward. "I did an underwater dive last year when we took our vacation in Tahiti. Maybe I could . . ."

"Pool dive?" Dad asked.

Mr. Shift frowned. "Well, we spent most of the time in the resort swimming pool. But then we went out in the ocean and swam down to look at the coral formations and the fish."

Dad sighed and shook his head. "It's a brave offer, Dennis, but I need to concentrate on what I'm doing. Not worry about a beginning diver."

Suddenly Dad's head gave a little jerk. Then . . .

He looked straight at me. "Kent. Looks like it's just you and me, son. Let's go!"

24

I guess I should have been scared. After all, I'd never been on a night dive in my life.

I guess I should have been nervous. Sure, I'd gone to the classes with Dad. But those were just training—this was real!

For some reason I didn't feel scared or nervous, either one. I just handed Duke's reins to Mr. Aikman and marched down to help Pete take some of the lead out of his weight belt.

Maybe it was the way Dad's shoulders went back and the way that big smile lit up his face when he said: "It's just you and me, son."

I don't know what it was, but I wasn't the least bit worried. Well . . . I guess I was . . . but not about myself. The only thing that worried me was Mrs. Baum. Jordan said she didn't answer the last time he signaled her. If we didn't hurry . . .

Greg and Dad lifted the tank so I could put my arms through the harness. Pete tried to tighten the straps on his fins so they wouldn't fall off my feet. But with just one hand he didn't have much luck.

Once my tank was on and all snugged down, Dad and Greg adjusted them.

Side by side, we strolled into the lake, stopped about waist deep, and put on our fins.

"Better move the horses uphill," Dad called. "We start pulling these ropes, the sound of them rattling and sliding through the grass might spook them. Wait until Kent and I have our ends tied before you wrap your ends around the saddle horns."

The fathers walked over to get on the horses, but Mr. Aikman stopped them.

"The boys know their mounts better than you do," he said. "Besides that, they're better riders. We'll handle the horses. You guys take care of the ropes for us."

Each of the men found a rope. They'd feed the line out so we wouldn't have so much weight to drag in the water. Then, once the ropes were tied on, they'd take the other end to their sons.

"Ready!" Dad called.

Greg trotted out and handed him the ends of the four ropes on the left. Pete gave me the four on the right.

"We'll swim out before we start down," he told me. "I'll tie. You hold the light for me. When I'm ready for the other four ropes, I'll wave."

I nodded.

Dad looked at Greg. "Once we get our ends tied on, we'll swim aside and let you start the boys. Be sure everyone is out from between these ropes. Rowdy!" he yelled up the hill. "Don't let the horses get the ropes tangled around their legs. If they get to pulling too hard and rear up, they could fall over backward and the boys—"

"Simon," Mr. Aikman called back. "The boys and I know what we're doing. You take care of your end. We'll do our job up here."

Dad nodded, then he smiled over at me.

"Keep the light on where I'm tying. When we're done, we'll come up. Okay?"

"Okay."

"Let's get 'er done."

We slipped our masks on, cleared the regulators, and—a light in one hand and four ropes in the other—we swam for the submarine.

The water was cloudy, but with the powerful lights I could still see the bottom. As we moved farther from shore, deeper, the muddy bottom disappeared into nothingness. I stayed with Dad, though, and never gave it a thought. One handful of rope and the other holding the light made swimming a little tricky, at first. But after a few feet I got the hang of guiding with my fins and my body.

What I noticed the most was the quiet.

Above—even when Dad was giving instructions and everyone was quiet—it wasn't really quiet. There was the constant hum of the light generator. There were the sounds of horses stomping their hooves and snorting. Men moving about. Crickets chirping. The breeze rustling the leaves.

Here—except for my own breathing—there was silence. Nothing but a peaceful stillness.

Then . . .

I saw it.

About ten feet below us and a little to the left, a dark form began to take shape through the murky water. Round and tapered, like the body of a big fish—an enormous shark—it lay motionless on the bottom. I knew what it was, but seeing it for the first time gave me an eerie feeling. Lifeless and still, I could almost picture a sudden movement. A quick flip of a fin or tail that would bring it to life. Send it knifing through the water and . . .

Suddenly I realized I was holding my breath. I forced myself to concentrate. Breathe slow and steady.

Dad swam to the propeller on the back of the sub. The prop was quite a bit bigger than those I'd seen on an outboard motor. The guard around it was probably three to four feet around and attached to the back of the sub with four steel rods. Tucking three of the ropes under his arm, and dropping his light, Dad tied the fourth to the propeller guard. Once done, he pulled on it, then yanked a couple of times to make sure the knot was secure.

Careful to keep it from glaring in his eyes, I held my light on where he worked. Dad finished all four of his ropes, then he waved for me to bring mine. When all eight ropes were tied, he picked up his light from the bottom and swam around to the front of the submarine. I wanted to follow him. I wanted to inspect the thing, see what it looked like, how it was made.

That could wait.

Dad pointed his light at the front of the sub for a moment or two, then pointed up. I met him on the surface.

"It's Mrs. Baum, all right," he told me, once he had the hose out of his mouth. "She's unconscious, but still responsive."

I pulled my hose out. "What's that mean, Dad?"

He smiled. "Her eyes are closed, but when the light hit her, she flinched. It means she's still alive, but we need to hurry.

"Rowdy?"

"Ready, Simon!"

"You'll have to pull toward the fence and the light generator. If you go the other way, we'll get tangled in the tree again."

"Will do," Mr. Aikman called back. "Want us to start?"

"Just a second." Dad turned to me. "I'll go down where I can see the ropes. You stay here and watch. If anything starts to come loose, I'll hit you with my light. You yell at them to stop, okay?"

"Yes, sir."

"Rowdy!" he shouted. "Count to ten, then start pulling. If Kent yells—stop."

"Got ya, Simon."

Floating on the surface like a jellyfish, I kept my light on Dad. I could barely see him when he stopped. I knew he was aiming his light on the ropes at the back of the sub, only the water was so cloudy I couldn't see that far. Every muscle tight and tense, I watched. Waited.

Then . . . ever so slowly at first . . . Dad's light started to move.

I followed from above as we headed in.

I stayed even with him. In a little while I could see him clearly in my light. A few more feet and the outline—the shape of the sub—began to appear. It was still ominous and eerie-looking. Then I could see the propeller guard and the ropes.

Finally I saw the muddy bottom as the sub slid closer and closer to the shore.

Before I knew it, Dad was on the surface with me. We swam along, watching the ropes. Every now and then Dad would raise his head to see if the hatch was above the surface.

When the wheel and the very top of the hatch port were a good two inches above the waterline, Dad ripped off his mask.

"That's good, boys. Hold it!"

Wriggling his shoulders, he got out of his tank and handed it to me. My fins brushed the bottom, but it wasn't quite shallow enough to stand up. Holding his tank, I treaded water and watched as he climbed on top of the thing and started turning the wheel.

It moved a lot easier than I expected. Then he gave it a hard spin and lifted.

"Emma? Emma Baum? Can you hear me? Emma?"

He stood up on the back of the sub and reached out toward me. "Tank. Quick."

I handed it to him. He yanked the hose and regulator off, twisted the valve all the way open. Then, holding the tank in front of him, he kind of dived at the hatch. The only thing left were his legs.

Suddenly Greg was there with us.

"What's he doing?" I asked.

"Flooding the compartment with air. All the oxygen's used up. Got to get fresh air in there so—"

Dad yelled something. Hanging upside down in the opening, we couldn't understand him.

"What?" Greg called.

"The other tank!"

Greg helped me out of my tank. Like Dad had done, he yanked the hose from the regulator and climbed up on the sub. Before he handed it down alongside where Dad was hanging, he opened the valve. I could hear the air spewing out.

Then another sound came to my ears. It was a siren. Glancing toward the dam, I saw the second ambulance racing across.

"Emma." I could barely hear Dad's voice. "Come on, hon. Wake up."

There was no response. Just the scream of the siren, howling in the distance.

"Emma." His voice was louder now. Determined and almost angry. "Open your eyes, Emma! Wake up!"

We'd tried so hard. Everyone. We had worked together. We'd done the very best we could. But what if all we'd done was for nothing?

What if we were too late?

25

Eyes squeezed so tight that it made my head ache, I could hear the words inside my skull:

"Please let her be all right. Please don't let her die."

I blinked and looked up. I could hear Dad's voice. I treaded water. *Please.* And waited. *Please help her.* And watched. And suddenly Greg straightened up. He looked down at me and smiled.

With him out of the hole, I could hear Dad talking to Mrs. Baum.

"No. Don't try to get up. You're safe. We've got you. Just sit there for a moment. Let us help you."

Feet kicking and struggling, Dad backed himself out of the hole.

"Oxygen," he whispered.

Greg leaped from the back of the sub and sprinted to shore. There was a whole lot of movement on the bank that I hadn't even noticed before. Mr. Aikman had ridden Duke to the gate and was leading the ambulance through the pasture. The guys were off their horses, leading them out of the way while their dads moved the ropes.

Greg was in the back of the ambulance before it rolled to a complete stop. By the time they turned the siren off and hopped out, he already had the little green oxygen tank and was racing for the lake. The two men followed him, but about halfway to me, one doubled back to get the ladder.

I swam out of the way and sloshed up to join my friends.

We all watched as Dad took the oxygen tank and squeezed down into the sub. For the life of me, I couldn't figure how. The thing looked barely big enough for one person to fit inside, much less two.

While we waited, a flash of light caught my eye. I glanced to the dead-end road that led to Mrs. Baum's house. Three more cars drove up and stopped beside where the men had parked. It was hard to see past the floodlights on the generator. But when one of the doors opened, I saw someone with long hair. When she stepped out, I could tell it was a woman wearing a dress.

"Looks like Samantha's wedding shower is over," I told Ted. "Guess our moms are coming to see what's going on."

The men must have noticed, too. They scurried over to where they'd left their clothes and started trying to sort things out and find their trousers.

By the time we all gathered by the base of the fallen cottonwood tree, it was probably one of the weirdest-looking groups anyone could imagine. There were eight boys in their bathing trunks. Eight women in formal dresses—who still had on their makeup and jewelry. And seven gentlemen wearing dress slacks with no shirts or shoes.

If some stranger had happened on to the scene, without any idea of what was going on, the poor guy would have probably fainted, just from the sight.

Mrs. Baum's head finally appeared from the hatch. Slow and careful, they helped her out. Greg held on to her until Dad climbed out. Then they lowered her to the other two firefighters. They carried her to shore, where Pete and Mr. Bently had the stretcher waiting.

"I'm fine," Mrs. Baum protested when they carried the stretcher toward the ambulance. "I've just got a little headache, but other than that I'm fine. Let me off this fool thing. I just want to go home and rest. I don't know what all the fuss is about, but—"

"Emma!" Dad's voice was kind yet firm when he caught up with them. "We need to have a doctor check you over. Make sure you're all right."

"But—"

"No *buts*. You're going to the hospital. They may even keep you overnight."

"But—"

"We'll watch the house. Make sure nobody bothers anything."

"But—" She tried to sit up.

Mom came to stand beside Dad when they put her into the back of the ambulance. "Emma. Just calm down and quit your fussing."

Greg leaned over and whispered something to Dad. He nodded and whispered to Mom. She smiled.

"Tell you what, Emma. Why don't I ride with you to the emergency room," Mom said. "There's enough space back here. I'll just go along for the ride. Make sure they treat you right, while you're there."

The old woman's eyes kind of lit up. She leaned back on the stretcher and seemed to relax a bit.

"Still think it's a bunch of nonsense," she muttered. "I don't need to go to see no fool doctor. But if you're going with me . . . well, I guess . . ."

Mom climbed in the back and sat down on the bench next to her. One of the other paramedics climbed in next to them. Greg and Dad told Pete to ride in front with the driver. At the open doorway he hesitated.

"I don't need no fool doctor to tell me my arm's broken," Pete teased.

Both men glared at him. They looked at each other, smiled, and shoved him into the ambulance.

"Oh, sit down and shut up," both said with a chuckle.

Greg closed the door. "Might call dispatch. See if Captain Miller can send a wrecker or two to get the truck out that you messed up."

"*I* messed up?" Pete yelped. "Hey, that wasn't my fault."

Greg shrugged. "You were driving."

Pete kind of sneered at him and gave a quick gesture with his good hand. Then he leaned to the side so he could see around Greg and Dad.

"Hey, where's Kent?" he asked.

"I'm right here, Pete," I called.

He waved me over. I trotted over to them. Pete reached out with his good arm and ruffled my hair.

"Good job, kid. If you hadn't come up with the idea of using the horses, we might not have gotten her out of there in time."

"Thanks, Pete."

As they drove slowly up the hill, so as not to jostle Mrs. Baum too much, Dad, Greg, and I walked back to join the rest of our group. Before we reached the others, Dad stepped in front of me.

He turned to face me and stuck out his hand. Not quite knowing what to do, I put my hand out, too. Dad shook it.

"I'm proud of you, Kent," he said softly. "I know that was your first night dive. It's pretty scary for most people. But you acted like an old pro. You did a good job, son."

I don't know what made me prouder—what Dad said, or the way he shook my hand and smiled at me.

Greg looked down his nose at me. He arched an eyebrow and shook his head.

"Hey, punk. Don't expect me to go braggin' about how brave you were. You didn't do nothing more than what I expected from you, all along. Ain't no big deal."

He stood there and glared at me a second. Then a smile curled the corners of his mouth. All of a sudden those big arms of his wrapped around me. He gave me such a hug, I thought he was going to squeeze the air clean out of me.

All three of us—side by side—strolled up to join the others.

Everyone stood around and visited for a time. We took turns explaining to the moms all that had happened. Told them about Jordan hearing the SOS, and how we located the sub. Then there were theories and guesses about where and how Mrs. Baum got the submarine and *why* she was out in the lake in the thing . . . and so much noise . . . well, all I could think about was how quiet and peaceful it was when I was underwater with Dad.

After a time we got the rest of the flashlights from our fishing camp and showed the moms the boathouse and the trench that led to the lake. Then everyone wanted to inspect the submarine. Dad handed Ted one of the big underwater lights. The women, dressed in high heels and fancy dresses, decided not to go sloshing out into the lake. They headed back to the cars and went home. Our dads stayed with us. Once the women left, the men stripped down to their underwear. Ted and his dad went first. They circled the submarine, then took turns climbing through the hatch to check out the insides. Everyone else sort of paired off and waited his turn. It was almost time for Jordan and me to go look it over when the wrecker showed up.

The dads were worse than us kids when it came to watching the wrecker. Not even bothering to put their slacks on, they trotted up the hill. The guy in the wrecker said he was afraid to drag the truck out because it might bend the driveshaft. Then he aimed his flashlight down into the trench and looked underneath the EMS truck.

"Already bent," he announced. "Might as well drag 'er out of there."

Only his truck wasn't strong enough, so he had to call for a second wrecker to come and help. By the time they were done, it was almost light enough to see without the generator. There had been so much going on, I didn't even feel like I'd been up all night. I wasn't the least bit sleepy or tired.

Now that all the excitement was over, the men helped us break camp and load our things to take home. We'd try the all-night fishing trip another time. Mr. Aikman told Ted and me to go check the bank poles.

"Not right to leave fish dangling on a hook," he said. "Any worth keeping, we'll clean. Otherwise, make sure all the bait is off and the hooks are tied so they won't snag anything."

When we got back, most everybody had gone. Greg, Dad, and Mr. Aikman were still there, gathering up our ropes.

"We'll put these back in the garage," Dad said. "Then we'll have Greg drive us home. Soon as I take a shower, we'll go check on your mom and Mrs. Baum. Kent, you want to grab that last rope over there?"

Beside the dirt-covered ball of roots at the base of the big cottonwood, I picked up the rope and started wrapping it around my arm.

A little orange sliver of the morning sun peeked above the oak trees on the back side of Mrs. Baum's house. If I hadn't been standing right there at that very instant—if I hadn't bent over to pick up the rope, just when I did—I would have never seen it.

A bright flash. Less than an inch around. It glistened and sparkled at me from the dirt. Hit me smack in the eye.

26

Dad and I both took showers. He had me go first so he could shave. When we finished and dressed, we dropped Greg off at the fire department. Then Dad and I drove to the hospital to check on Mom and Mrs. Baum.

We could hear Mrs. Baum's fussing before we even opened the door to her room. "Isn't this just like a hospital. Doctor *finally* says it's okay to go home, then you sit around and wait for three hours. Takes them forever to get the paperwork done. If I had any sense, I'd just up and march out of this place and let them hunt for me. I'd just . . ."

Dad shoved the door open and walked in. Mrs. Baum sat in a wheelchair beside the hospital bed. Mom was in a straight-back chair beside her.

"Hi, Emma," Dad greeted. "How you feeling?"

"Oh"—she smiled—"I'm fine. Told that fool doctor there wasn't nothing wrong with me. Young whippersnapper still made me sit here for three hours. Said he wanted to watch me." She shook her head. "Don't know what he was watching. All

I was doing was sittin' here, waitin' to go home."

Mom smiled and shot Dad a quick wink. Mrs. Baum kind of leaned to the side so she could see who was following Dad into her room. When she spotted me, a smile lit up her wrinkled old face.

"Hello, Kent. Your mom says you and Jordan were the ones who found me. Saved my life. I almost made it back to the dock, when *whack*. That old tree pounced on me and pinned me to the bottom. I surely do appreciate you and those other boys. I'd still be sittin' in that submersible if it hadn't been for you."

"Talking about the sub . . ." Dad sat on the edge of the bed. "Where in the world did that thing come from? And why were you in it? And . . ."

It was at least another hour before the nurses came and finally told Mrs. Baum she could go home. After an hour of talking and answering questions—that, plus the drive home—I learned a whole bunch about Mrs. Baum and the submarine and mining.

Mr. Baum was a miner. I remembered her telling us that, the day Mom made me go with her for a visit. But I always figured he was a coal miner. Only Mr. Baum wasn't really a miner. He was what they called a troubleshooter—a guy who solved problems they had with mine-shaft construction, poisonous gas, or flooding. He must have been good at it, too, because he worked for a number of big mining companies all the way from California and Nevada to Alaska. They weren't coal mines, either. They were gold mines.

About a year before he was to retire, one of the big mines in British Columbia, Canada, started flooding. The geologists decided it was from a nearby lake and called Mr. Baum in.

The mining company bought the submarine from the Canadian government. They got it for practically nothing. That's because it was an experimental two-man sub. Trouble was, with two people in it, a gas-operated engine, and oxygen to breathe, they could only carry enough gasoline to stay down for about fifteen minutes. They were getting ready to turn the thing into scrap and start over again when the mining company bought it.

Mr. Baum took out the gas tank and motor and replaced it with a smaller electric engine. The marine batteries could go for twelve to twenty-two hours without being recharged. Making it a one-man sub instead of two, left room for enough compressed air to stay down for eight hours or more.

After Mr. Baum found where the mine shaft was

leaking and showed them how to repair it, he asked if he could have the sub.

"But why?" Mom asked as we drove across the dam. Mrs. Baum rode shotgun, next to Dad in the front seat. She turned a bit so she could see Mom and smiled.

"As soon as we get to the house, I'll show you."

Even from behind her, I could see her stiffen when we turned off the road and into our driveway, instead of taking her straight home.

"Why are we stopping?"

"Kent found something you might like to have," Dad said. "He'll hurry."

I leaped out of the car, and Dad tossed me the keys. Once inside, I turned off the alarm, grabbed my backpack, and raced to the car.

"What's in the pack?" Mrs. Baum asked.

"I want to see what you're going to show us, first," I said.

We heard the table saw as soon as Dad pulled into her driveway and turned off the engine. Mrs. Baum hopped out and toddled around to the front of her house to see what was going on. We followed her.

Ted and his dad were just putting the finishing touches on the door frame. The new door leaned against the wall.

"Rowdy, what are you doing?"

Mr. Aikman explained about busting the door open the night before, when she didn't answer. He said that since he was the one who broke it, he thought he should replace it. Mrs. Baum told him the thing was old and about halfway rotted, anyway, and that she intended to pay for the door and his time.

I guess they would have argued, back and forth, for the rest of the day if I hadn't stepped between them.

"Mrs. Baum?" I said politely. "Wasn't there something you were going to show us?"

She blinked. "Oh, yeah. Come on in the house."

"Can Ted come, too?"

She shrugged. "Might as well. I promised my husband, Jeb, that I would keep it a secret. After last night everyone's seen the submarine. Ain't a secret if the whole country knows about it. Come on."

We all followed her through the house and into her kitchen. Mrs. Baum opened the freezer and dug around inside. "Sorry I don't have any pie or cake to offer," she said over her shoulder. "If you boys will drop by this afternoon or tomorrow, I'll have some chocolate chip cookies baked up for you. Y'all take a seat. Make yourselves comfortable."

We sat in the chairs around the kitchen table. Mrs. Baum set a tin container full of flour on the counter.

"She going to fix the cookies *now*?" I whispered. Ted shrugged. Mom shushed me.

Mrs. Baum dug deeper into the freezer and pulled out another tin. Then she got a bowl from the shelf and carefully dumped that container into it. It didn't sound like flour when it hit the metal bowl. I could hear it *clink* and *clunk*. Then she started digging through it with her hand, pulling something out of the flour.

"My father found these, down in the Bottom, just about the time they were finishing construction on the lake dam. Family farm was six hundred and forty acres. Went from the eighty up behind the house, down across the valley, and halfway up the Point. County bought the front part of the place for the lake. Dad had more or less retired from dairy farming and didn't need the land. But the farm had been in the family since his grandfather homesteaded the place.

"Guess Dad was taking one more look at that part of the old farm before the lake covered it up. That's when he stumbled on to this."

She turned on the faucet and started rinsing whatever it was she'd dug out of the flour. When she was done, Mrs. Baum turned around and handed each one of us a piece of shiny rock.

The one she gave me was about the size of Dad's thumb. Mom held one that filled her whole hand. I looked at mine. Twisted it between my fingers. It was bright and sparkly, like light bouncing off ripples on the lake.

Mr. Aikman gasped. "Silver."

"Your dad found a silver mine?" Mom asked.

Mrs. Baum shook her head. "That's what Dad thought. He put a little piece of it in a box and mailed it to us while we were in Alaska. Jeb knew what it was right off, but he took it in to have the assayer make sure.

"It's platinum. High-grade platinum, at that. What you're looking at isn't even ore. Those are pure platinum nuggets that my father found."

The grown-ups gasped. I looked at my chunk again. It was pretty, all right. But I still didn't see what all the fuss was about. I leaned over toward Mom.

"What's platinum?" I whispered.

"It's a valuable metal. They use it for jewelry and stuff like that. It's worth a lot of money."

"More than gold?" I whispered.

Mom looked me square in the eye. When she nodded, I felt my head kind of snap back.

"More than gold."

27

Mrs. Baum had Mom help her get some glasses from the cabinet. She had a big pitcher of lemonade in the fridge. Once everyone had something to drink, she went on with her story.

"The mail service was better in those days than it is now," Mrs. Baum said. "Still took three weeks to get the package. Along with it came a letter saying Dad had been using a pick and shovel, and had already tunneled about four feet into the rock. Said it was starting to look like a real, honest-to-goodness mine. The package and letter got to us on a Friday afternoon, so Jeb had to wait until Monday to get it down to the assay office. As soon as he had the report, he called to have Dad be sure and write down *exact* directions to where he was digging. Only nobody answered the phone when he called."

Mrs. Baum hesitated, her eyes kind of drifting off to gaze up at the ceiling for a moment, then looked back at us.

"The reason there was no answer . . . that's when

Dad and Al Beckman had their car wreck. Mother was at the hospital. That's why no one answered . . . and . . ." She sort of drifted off again, then cleared her throat. "Anyway, Mother called us that evening, and we hopped a plane the next morning. Got here about two hours before Dad passed away."

We all sat quiet for a time. Dad handed his piece of rock back to Mrs. Baum.

"So you never knew where he'd found the platinum."

She shook her head. "The lake was already about three-fourths of the way up the ridge. All Mother could tell us was"—she pointed with a wave of her hand, toward the point—"'I heard him tapping, with that pickax, down yonder.'

"Jeb and I moved here when he retired. Mother needed someone around, but she just didn't have any reason to live without Dad. She passed away the following summer.

"Working around gold mines and gold miners, Jeb knew how greedy people can be. He figured if someone saw a submersible in this part of the country, there would be lots of questions. He also knew there'd be a swarm of people all over that lake looking for the mine. Most of them without the slightest idea what they were doing. Probably end up getting hurt or getting someone drowned. So he rented a bulldozer and dug the trench before the lake was full. Built the work shed to store and keep the batteries charged and hide the compressor and the air tanks. Bought bridge timbers for the top and put dirt and grass over them to hide it. And spent the next twelve years looking for that mine."

"That's why you didn't want us riding in front of your house, isn't it?" Ted asked. "Because we might find those bridge timbers."

Mrs. Baum shook her head. "Not so much that you might find them. I knew those timbers were old. I was afraid a horse might bust through or break a leg. Didn't want any of you boys getting hurt."

Dad took a long sip of his lemonade and propped his elbows on the table. "Was that what sent him to the nursing home, Emma?" he asked. "Did he get trapped in the sub, like you did, and couldn't get air?"

"No. We always carried a spare mask and scuba tank in the event that something went wrong with the sub. We never had to use it. I had it on, last night, but with that darned tree sittin' on top of me, I couldn't get the hatch open. Did give me enough extra air for you to find me and get me out, though.

"No, Jeb was just fixing his coffee one morning. I heard the crash when he fell and came running. Had a massive stroke. That's what the doctors said. Old age. Nothing more. Nothing less."

"But why did *you* start taking the sub out, Emma?" Mom asked. "Sounds like it was your husband's job, not yours."

"I didn't take it out." She gave a little snort. "I just let it sit in the boathouse. Left the fool contraption there for about eight years. Between Jeb's retirement check and the platinum Dad had stashed, things were fine. Then that darned nursing home . . ." She paused a moment and gave another little snort. "Well, not just *that* nursing home—all of them. They all started going up on their prices. Every two to three months I'd get another letter telling me how much more it was going to cost the following month. What you're holding in your hands is the last of the platinum. When that's gone . . . well, it costs over three thousand dollars a month. Jeb's retirement won't cover it, and the only other thing I can do is start selling off the farm."

She sighed and stared off through the window.

"For the life of me, I don't know why I got such a problem with that. I can't farm it. Jeb and I never had any children, so there's nobody to leave it to.

It's just . . . just . . . well, it's my home. I grew up here. When he retired, Jeb and I had twelve of the best years of our life—right here. Just hate the thought of selling it and moving to a little apartment in town."

Something clunked me on the knee. It wasn't hard enough to hurt, but it made me jump. Then it clunked me again. This time it did hurt.

I peeked under the table. Dad's boot came flying at my leg a third time. I managed to move just in time to keep from getting kicked again.

Frowning, I looked up at him. He winked and nodded toward my backpack, which I had laid carefully in the corner. I smiled, realizing what he was trying to tell me, then hopped up and went to get it.

"Maybe this will help, Mrs. Baum."

I put the pack on the table and unzipped it. Then, using both hands, I reached inside.

Mom and Dad smiled when I put the heavy jar on the table. Mrs. Baum, Mr. Aikman, and Ted just sat there with their mouths gaping open.

When I brought it to the house, early this morning, Dad told me it was a gallon-size Mason jar. Part of the rubber seal was still around the top. The rest had rotted and fallen away. The wire bale that latched it was so rusted that it would probably fall apart if you so much as blew on it. But inside . . .

"Oh, my gosh!" Mrs. Baum gasped.

She let out a little laugh. I glanced at her and saw the big smile on her face. I also saw a tear roll down her cheek. Ever so slowly, as if nearing something magic or forbidden, she reached out a trembling hand and touched it with the tips of her fingers. Then she drew her hand back and reached again.

"It's Grandpa's silver dollars."

The jar looked like it was ready to fall apart, but the coins inside were just as bright and shiny as the day they were made. Mrs. Baum wiped her cheek.

"Where on earth . . ."

"It was all wrapped up in the roots of that old cottonwood tree that fell on the sub."

"No wonder we couldn't ever find them." She gave a little laugh. "I bet that tree was just a sapling when Grandpa buried them. Big as it is, we would have had to dig the whole tree up. I'll be . . ."

Dad reached over and patted Mrs. Baum's hand. "There's not just silver dollars in that jar, Emma. Greg Ratcliff, a man who works with me at the fire department, used to collect coins when he was a kid. We didn't open it because we wanted you to be the first. But just from looking through the jar, he said there are silver dollars, five-dollar gold pieces, twenty-dollar gold pieces, and something he called

a Double Eagle. He told me to make sure you
knew not to spend so much as a penny of it until
he brought his book out and went through them
with you. He also said . . ." Dad wiggled her hand
in his. "Emma, you listening?"

"Yes, Simon."

"He also said you need to put them in a safety-
deposit box at the bank—*today*! Just from looking
through the jar at the dates and what little he could
see around the sides, Greg said you probably had
over a hundred thousand dollars' worth of coins in
there."

Mrs. Baum's mouth fell open. But she didn't say
anything. Instead, she started crying, then laughing, then crying some more.

"I don't think you'll have to worry about keeping your husband in the nursing home anymore,"
Mom said, giving her a big hug.

Mrs. Baum hugged her back. Then she hugged
Dad. Then she turned to me. "Thank you, Kent.
Thank you so much."

I let her hug me.

"Remember when you asked me what Krissi and
I were talking about the other night?" She whispered it right in my ear, making sure no one else
could hear.

"Yes," I whispered back.

"We were talking about you. She thinks you're really cute. But don't tell anybody I told you."

I felt the heat rush to my cheeks. I hugged her back and smiled.

The more I thought about it, that hug from Mrs. Baum was probably one of the nicest, best hugs I ever had in my life.

I remember thinking what a grouch she was— just a nasty old lady who did nothing but scream at little kids for riding across her land. I remember being about halfway scared of her. So scared that I was afraid to tell her off or call her names like I wanted to. I remember Mom practically dragging me to her house that day, and how I decided she wasn't quite as bad as I thought. Besides, she made great chocolate chip cookies. She had a mischievous side, too. Her eyes sparkled when she told me the secret about Krissi.

When she hugged me, her cheek was wet. The sleeve of her blouse was damp from her crying.

But it was totally awesome.

I mean . . . never been hugged by a monster before.

It wasn't too bad.

About the Author

BILL WALLACE grew up in Oklahoma. Along with riding their horses, he and his friends enjoyed campouts and fishing trips. Toasting marshmallows, telling ghost stories to scare one another, and catching fish was always fun.

One of the most memorable trips took place on the far side of Lake Lawtonka, at the base of Mt. Scott. He and his best friend, Gary, spent the day shooting shad with bow and arrows, cutting bank poles, and getting ready to go when their dads got home from work.

Although there was no "monster" in Lake Lawtonka, one night there *was* a "sneak attack" by a rather large catfish tail. Checking the bank poles was not nearly as fun or "free" after that point, but it was the inspiration for this story.

Bill Wallace is now a full-time author, but for many years he was the principal and physical education teacher at an elementary school in Chickasha,

Oklahoma. He has won nineteen children's state awards, and been awarded the Arrell Gibson Lifetime Achievement Award for Children's Literature from the Oklahoma Center for the Book.

HOW MANY OF THESE GREAT ANIMAL STORIES HAVE YOU READ?

TOTALLY DISGUSTING!
0-671-75416-5

UPCHUCK AND THE ROTTEN WILLY
0-671-01415-3

UPCHUCK AND THE ROTTEN WILLY: THE GREAT ESCAPE
0-671-01937-6

UPCHUCK AND THE ROTTEN WILLY: RUNNING WILD
0-7434-0027-5

BY NIKKI WALLACE

STUBBY AND THE PUPPY PACK
0-671-02589-9

STUBBY AND THE PUPPY PACK TO THE RESCUE
0-7434-2694-0 (hardcover)
0-7434-2695-9 (paperback)